Three Music Stories from Maine

Edward Judd

Creative Music Productions—Auburn, ME
ISBN: 979-8-3302-5575-7
eBook ISBN: 979-8-3302-5577-1
Title: *Three Music Stories from Maine*
Author: Edward Judd
Digital distribution | 2024
Paperback | 2024

*Acknowledgement:
Edited Abenaki Dictionary; Michael Forbes Wilcox;
http://www.mfw.us › blog › uploads › 2020/04

Published in the United States by New Book Authors Publishing

Dedication

To my wife, Irene, who keeps me going

Preface

Let me be honest from the start. This is my first foray into fiction writing. The three stories have common elements. One, they take place in Maine, where I have lived for more than 35 years (yes, the locals still consider me a newcomer). Two, the main character is a music educator (or will become one), and many scenes in the stories are based on my experiences as a music teacher during my 46 year career, although music is not mentioned through the first four chapters. In fact, a lot of this I could have written as a memoir, but as fiction, I can play with some of the facts and embellish as I see fit. Some of you who know me may find it interesting to speculate if certain scenes are truly fictional, or if they actually took place. One thing I can tell you. In "Transitions of a Band Director," the conversation between the main character and the Principal where they talk about performance aesthetics before the festival trip NEVER takes place in a typical high school.

I originally set out to write short stories, but these three stories are a bit too long to be considered short stories, they would probably be classified as novellas.

I am grateful to my former students, fellow educators, and others that have helped shape my experiences. I am also grateful to my family for their encouragement throughout this process.

-EJ

Three Music Stories from Maine
TABLE OF CONTENTS

Soulmate Lost

Chapter 1
THAT Dream and the Dancing Lights

"A soulmate is someone to whom we feel profoundly connected, as though the communicating and communing that take place between us were not the product of intentional efforts, but rather a divine grace." — Thomas Moore

Phillip woke up with a start. It was unusual, but it was THAT dream again. One experienced multiple times going back to when he was a toddler. Now, only a couple of weeks shy of his eleventh birthday, he had become very familiar with the girl in his dreams. She was Asian with straight black hair that ended just below the shoulders. She had bangs and wore a modest white dress. She sat on a wall, sometimes stone, sometimes brick. Sometimes, Phillip would sit next to her on the wall, and sometimes he would stand. Sometimes she would speak to him, and sometimes, not. Other times, they would laugh together about something, although Phillip could not remember exactly what. That, of course, led to the features about her that Phillip found most endearing. She had the kindest eyes that he had ever seen on anyone, and her smile was genuine, caring and extremely beautiful. But what Phillip found so uncanny was the feelings he experienced each time he would dream about her. He would wake up to a feeling of calm that he rarely experienced, along with major feelings of contentment, and the feeling that all was right with the world. Each time he would dream about her, he would look forward to the next time she would appear, as if her presence was a cerebral security blanket.

He stared at the lamp sitting on the table next to his bed. It reminded him of his first dream of her. As a toddler, Phillip had been experiencing night terrors. In those days, Mom or Dad would put him to bed and then close the door to his bedroom. He would drift off to sleep, but later would wake up to a terrifying sight. White lights, dancing on the ceiling, waving back and forth in an undiscernible pattern and then dashing out of sight, followed by a similar set of lights. Young Phillip didn't understand what was happening. Later, he would discover that the dancing lights were made by the headlights of vehicles passing the house. But to a three or four-year-old, it was very disturbing, and more than once Phillip's parents would be awakened by his screams.

That was when she first appeared to him. She said, "Don't be afraid."

Perhaps it was that she was new to him, and therefore Phillip found it difficult to trust her. But her words led Phillip to cope and reason that the dancing lights would not cause him harm. One day, he saw that his mother was preparing to throw away an old desk lamp, and that sparked an idea. Phillip begged her to set the lamp up next to his bed. She granted his request, and every night thereafter, Phillip would turn the lamp on as he went to bed, and should he wake up during the night, the desk lamp would be a cherished ally in keeping the dancing lights at bay.

Chapter 2
The Messages

"People think a soul mate is your perfect fit, and that's what everyone wants. But a true soul mate is a mirror, the person who shows you everything that is holding you back, the person who brings you to your own attention so you can change your life." — Elizabeth Gilbert

She didn't always speak to him, but when she did, it was usually encouraging, occasionally a warning. But when each dream ended, there was always that beautiful smile and encouraging gaze. Even if she said nothing to him, she was a welcome sight.

Philip could vividly remember one such encounter with her, just at about the time that he was entering Kindergarten. She appeared to him and said, "Trust those who know."

Phillip wasn't sure what to think, but the following day in kindergarten class, he was able to make the connection. The task of the day was to arrange a collection of pegs on a pegboard in uniform-colored rows. All the red pegs in a row, all the blue pegs in a row, etc. To Phillip, it seemed easy enough, but every time he tried to insert a peg in the pegboard it wouldn't fit. No matter how hard he would try, Phillip could not make any of the pegs fit into the pegboard. He was frustrated and on the verge of tears when his cousin, Amelia, who was sitting next to him noticed what was happening. She seemed to know immediately what the problem was.

She said to him, "You have the wrong kind" and called to one of the students helping to pass out pegs and pegboards to come over to the table.

Philip said nothing while he allowed Amelia to take charge of the situation. She took Phillip's box of pegs and gave it to the girl saying, "These are large pegs, He needs a box of small ones."

The other girl took the box of large pegs back to the kindergarten teacher and returned with a different box. When Phillip saw the pegs in the other box, he immediately saw the difference in sizes, and realized that completing the assignment wouldn't be a problem. He was grateful to Amelia for helping him, but he also realized that Amelia's older sister had completed Kindergarten the year before, and that it was quite possible that her older sister had briefed Amelia on some of the things to expect in kindergarten. "Trust those who know." Now those words made sense.

Chapter 3
The Bullies

"Love is composed of a single soul inhabiting two bodies."— Aristotle

In Phillip's third grade year, he noticed something rather disturbing. It seemed as if the boys in his class were becoming more aggressive. Whether it was pushing and shoving in line on the way to recess or calling each other names when no adults were around. It was a departure from second grade year, when everyone seemed to get along quite well.

Eventually, a couple of these boys decided to target Phillip. Phillip was one of the bigger kids in the class. It was therefore quite satisfying for two of these bullies, both named Jake, that when they picked fights with Phillip, he didn't show any resistance. To Phillip, fighting was just wrong. It didn't serve any purpose, except to increase the aggressor's bragging rights, something that Phillip had no interest in. He also saw that it could spiral out of control among some kids, who ended up getting in trouble and the school would call in their parents to resolve the situation. However, the two Jakes were experienced bullies, keeping their aggression under control, and dedicating themselves to making Phillip's life as miserable as possible. Sometimes the abuse was verbal, sometimes physical, throwing punches to anywhere they could land on Phillip's body, always when there were no adults in sight. But Phillip could not bring himself to fight back, and sometimes he would end up in tears, to the delight of his tormentors.

Phillip didn't know what to do. When he tried to explain the situation to an adult, he would almost always be told "Hit back harder" or "Run away from those boys." He didn't consider either of those pieces of advice to be particularly practical. Then, one night, his dream girl appeared to him. For the first time that he could remember, she did not smile at him. She was stern and serious when she said to him, "You must fight." Phillip pondered her command for several days, then came a situation that made Phillip think of his dream girl's words.

Phillip and some of the neighborhood boys had gathered in his yard on a warm spring late afternoon. There were about a dozen boys who lived within walking distance from Phillip's house. They tended to hang together, sometimes getting into mischief together, but generally friendly to each other. They even formed a football team at one time with hopes of playing a group of boys in an adjoining neighborhood. On this day, they had gathered and were deciding what game they were going to play. All of a sudden, into the yard strode Meesha. Meesha was a boy who also lived down the street. He was about as old as Phillip, but he didn't appear to like Phillip very much. He would generally argue with anything that Phillip had to say or suggest. All the boys were quiet as Meesha walked up to Phillip and announced that he was going to fight him.

He looked Phillip right in the eye and menacingly said, "I'm going to kick your ass!"

Phillip blinked, but then several thoughts occurred to him at once. Although Meesha went to a different school, it appeared that he had somehow heard of Phillip's issues with the two Jakes and was now going to attempt to get Phillip to cry like the two Jakes did. That would certainly enhance Meesha's bragging rights in the neighborhood. However, Phillip also realized that this whole scene was absurd. The two Jakes had been trained in fighting. They would assume a standard boxer's stance with both fists in the proper position. As far as Phillip knew, Meesha, whose frame was considerably smaller than Phillip, had not had any such training. He then thought of his dream girl's words, and something just snapped. It was one thing to face two trained boxers, but for this punk, who Phillip realized was much more mouth than fists, to relent to Meesha was totally unacceptable. Meesha made the first move throwing a punch, but that's as far as he got.

Phillip started punching back, and just as it seemed that Meesha was starting to come to a major realization that he had totally miscalculated how this was going to turn out, Phillip grabbed him and threw him to the ground. Phillip continued to punch Meesha on the ground, and eventually some of the boys ended up pulling Phillip off Meesha. The rest of the boys pulled Meesha to his feet, who was now sporting a bloody nose. Phillip viewed Meesha's plight with no sympathy, which he was surprised at. It was unlike Phillip to view such a situation with little or no empathy. Some of the boys agreed to walk Meesha home, while Phillip bade farewell to the rest of the boys and headed inside his house.

Chapter 4
The Age Factor and the Crabs

"How every smile, every whisper brings me closer to the impossible conclusion that I have known you before, I have loved you before—in another time, a different place, some other existence."—Lang Leav

So, now on this night, just prior to his twelfth birthday, Phillip was once again visited by his dream girl. However, this time he noted something that he had not discerned in her previous visits. She seemed to be matching his age. When she first appeared to him, when he was little, she seemed about as old as Phillip was, about four years old. With tonight's visit, it would not be unreasonable to estimate her age at about eleven years old. Perhaps he would ask her about it the next time she appeared to him. In this evening's visit, she had another message for him. She said to him, "You do too much," another short message that Phillip had no idea what she was referring to.

He lay in bed and pondered about what that message could mean. He glanced at the clock. It was almost 4:30am on an early Sunday morning. In a couple of hours, he would have to start getting ready to go to church so he could sing with the youth choir at the 8 O'clock Mass. Every weekday, he again would have to arise early, put on that hated school uniform, and prepare for school. On Saturday, he also needed to get up early for youth basketball at the YMCA. He thought, "Wouldn't it be great to be able to sleep in one day and not have to go anywhere?"

As the weeks went on, and Phillip thought about the message more and more, he realized that getting up early every day was starting to take a toll on him. He wasn't getting as much sleep as he ought to and seemed to be getting tired a lot easier in the latter part of the day.

Finally, a solution presented itself. His membership in the YMCA was about to expire, and Phillip asked his mother not to renew his membership. He told her that he wanted to sign up for Little League, which would be starting in a few weeks, and that he didn't want to be involved in too many activities. His mother thought about it and agreed. From that point on, Phillip could sleep in on Saturdays for as long as he wanted.

As the summer progressed, Phillip would sometimes hang out with the other boys in the neighborhood, but also spent a lot of time alone. Much of his time would be spent at a beach located near his house. Colony Beach was about a 30-minute walk from Phillip's house, a walk that he was allowed to take on his own as long as he honored a promise made to his mother to never go swimming there. He regularly consulted a local tidal schedule before going there, and usually left his house precisely one hour before dead-low tide. The beach was small, probably less than two hundred feet long, although in Maine, such a small beach wasn't atypical. Maine has a long irregular coastline. To stretch it out into a single line, it would be almost 3,500 miles long, longer than the coast of California, and every other state except for Alaska, Florida, and Louisiana. But in many places, the coast was rocky, and inhospitable. Although beaches were fairly common along the southern end of the coastline in places such as Kennebunk, Ogunquit, York, and Old Orchard, they were rarer along the rest of the coastline. Phillip loved being at Colony beach. Standing at the water's edge, he could see three lighthouses warning boats away from hazards. On a nearby island, it seemed as if there were remnants of the foundation for a fourth lighthouse, although Phillip couldn't be sure.   Sometimes, as he gazed to the horizon, he might spot an oil tanker or cargo ship headed down the coast to Portland. But the feature of Colony Beach that Phillip really appreciated occurred during low tide. The ocean would recede to reveal several outcroppings of rocks and small sandbars. Scattered among the rocks and sandbars were several tidal pools, many of which held the promise of surprise. Digging clams in the sand bars was an activity that Phillip enjoyed. Sometimes, very small fish would get trapped in the tidal pools, although Phillip rarely came across them because the seagulls usually did a very professional job of finding them first. But sometimes, under pieces of seaweed in the tidal pools, Phillip would find other tiny wildlife. At first, it was mostly small crabs, baby rock crabs, but sometimes hermit crabs, that lived in a shell they carried on their backs. Phillip would bring paper cups with him. When he captured a crab, he would place it in a cup and fill the cup with seawater. He would also place a piece of seaweed in the cup which the crabs continued to use for cover, although there were times when he observed crabs munching on the seaweed as a food source. Sometimes he would take the cup containing a crab home with him. He started to build a small collection and started naming them. His first baby crab he named "Sandy," and his first hermit crab he called "Albert."

Phillip was quite fond of the collection of crabs at his house. He had built up a collection of seven or eight crabs, all of them in little paper cups, lined up in the family's screened-in porch on a shelf, complete with small paper signs on each cup displaying each crab's name. Then, one night, his dream girl appeared to him. He spoke to her, but she didn't really respond, only that beautiful smile and adoring look. She then said to him, "They must be free."

Phillip woke up.

He stared at the ceiling as he pondered the dream girl's words. This time, there was no mistaking what she was talking about. Phillip wasn't too thrilled about letting his crabs go. As far as he could tell, the crabs all seemed to be doing alright. He would replace sea water in the cups and seaweed on a regular basis. It was the first time he found himself questioning his dream girl. But the following day, his low tide adventure took an unexpected turn. When he arrived at the beach, the last remnants of high tide were receding. After a few minutes, he started on his usual hunt through the tidal pools. He approached a tidal pool and lifted a piece of seaweed to see what was underneath. Phillip was stunned when he found a tiny baby squid. He was astounded, and as he was contemplating what to do, the words of his dream girl came to mind. If it were a crab, he would have no problem adding it to his collection, but having no experience in taking care of a squid provided Phillip with some doubt about how well he would be able to properly care for this creature. After considerable thought, he took the piece of seaweed and placed it back over the baby squid in the tidal pool. Assuming the squid could continue to hide from predators, it had a chance at survival. In the days that followed, each day, Phillip would take one of his crabs back to the beach and set it free. He realized that as long as he kept them in a paper cup, they would not acquire any of the skills they would need to survive and avoid predators. As with the squid, he would place each crab in a tidal pool and cover it with seaweed. He was proud of his ability to amass a collection of crabs, but as his collection of crabs dwindled, he was also proud of his ability to adopt a more mature attitude.

Chapter 5
Avowing his Soulmate

"Eventually soulmates meet, for they have the same hiding place."— *Robert Brault*

Starting high school could be a very exciting time, and so it was for 14-year-old Phillip. New opportunities, new experiences, new challenges, it was like being given a 4-year blank slate to be filled with all sorts of experiences and achievements. So, Phillip started his high school experience finding out fairly quickly that high school was no utopia. Some of his teachers were likable enough, but some were not. Lunch period was almost an hour and a half long, with most of that time sitting in an algebra class, while the rest of the school took shifts at eating lunch. It really dragged his day down, and by the time he got to his last class of the day, English, he felt tired and couldn't concentrate very well. After the first few days, he joined the school band. Phillip had been cultivating his musical skills from a young age. Youth Choir, piano lessons, and other musical studies had brought him to the point where he wasn't afraid to display his talent. Unfortunately, the only opening that the band director had for Phillip was on the bass drum. No matter, he was confident that it wouldn't be long before he could move on to other instruments.

Phillip stared at the ceiling after the latest visit from his dream girl. He felt the usual feelings of euphoria that he felt each time she appeared to him. This night, she had looked at him adorably and said, "I am proud. Now you must follow your call."

Phillip didn't totally understand the message, but if past experience was a guide, understanding would come. He began to think about the way he regarded his dream girl. It seemed that he was feeling more affection for her. Perhaps it was because he was now a teenager, and much more interested in girls. And what wasn't there to like about this girl? Her beauty was a joy to behold, her affinity for Phillip and her level of caring were obvious, and her wisdom seemed impeccable. Was there any other girl out there that could even match up with her? Well, there was one fault with her. He didn't know if she actually existed. Was she an angel sent from afar? A figment of his imagination? A safe place for his mind to reside as it negotiated its way through the night? If she existed on this earth, could he possibly set out and find her? That sounded like a daunting task if ever there was one. If he could be sure she was real, he was certainly willing to undertake such a search. And yet, it seemed as if she were his best friend and perhaps even long-lost love from another existence all rolled into one. If she were real, he knew he might have difficulties relating to her and cultivating a relationship with her. In the real world, Phillip did not possess a high level of social skills with girls. But in his dreams, he felt so comfortable with this girl, he realized that his interaction with her was an enigma that may well be unattainable for him in the real world. This was soul-searching on a level that Phillip had never experienced before. He didn't know her name. She only appeared in his dreams, infrequently and unpredictably. Many times, she spoke in riddles. And yet, he felt such a high degree of closeness to her, an exemplary level of understanding and an incredible feeling of comfort in her presence, calling her his "dream girl" seemed so inadequate. There was only one logical conclusion. He would now think of her as his Soulmate.

Chapter 6
The Calling?

"Important encounters are planned by the soul long before the bodies see each other."

-Paulo Coelho

While it was true that Phillip was only a freshman band member, he had been making tremendous progress. He was holding his own with the older students, and with the school year little more than half over, and he had already learned the saxophone, was in the process of mastering the flute and was starting to learn the tuba. As spring arrived, the band was preparing to perform at a band festival, and by this time, Phillip had made enough progress on the tuba that he started playing it in band rehearsals. In fact, the director suggested to Phillip that he audition for the All-State Band. On this particular day, the band director seated Phillip next to Miles. Miles was a couple of years older than Phillip, and Phillip remembered him from a summer camp that they had both attended several years ago. They were working on a section of the music they would perform, and Miles was having difficulties. He just couldn't seem to play the rhythm correctly, and the display of his incompetence for all to see was getting him frustrated. It was beginning to sound like the band director was also getting frustrated, and Phillip wasn't far behind.

When the band director stopped rehearsal to work with another section of students, Phillip glanced over at the music Miles had. He thought, "Humph! plain off beats! Why is he having such problems with that?"

Phillip grabbed his own music off his stand and showed it to Miles. He said, "Look at my part! I play notes on the first and third beats of each measure."

He then pointed to the alto horn part that Miles was attempting to play. He continued, "You have notes on the second and fourth beat of each measure. What we have to do is take turns playing notes on every other beat."

Miles nodded as the band director started everyone on the same section of music once again. This time, Miles played his part perfectly, receiving compliments from the band director and from kids in the class. Phillip's pride was obvious. He had single handedly transformed Miles from failure to success. He then thought of his Soulmate's words, "Now you must follow your call."

Phillip wondered if perhaps that call lay in music. He had always had the feeling that he wanted to be a teacher when he grew up. In his elementary school days, he always thought he might want to be a history teacher, or maybe science. However, his experience with Miles seemed to open a new pathway, teaching music.

Chapter 7
The Dream Takes a Different Turn

"A soulmate is an ongoing connection with another individual that the soul picks up again in various times and places over lifetimes. We are attracted to another person at a soul level not because that person is our unique complement, but because by being with that individual, we are somehow provided with an impetus to become whole ourselves."
— Edgar Cayce

It was what many would consider a landmark moment of being a teenager. Getting one's driver's license. Mom had sent Phillip to driving school as a present for his sixteenth birthday. Ten weeks of evening classes, and another month of behind the wheel experience, and Phillip was sure he was ready for his test. He pretty much had the driver's manual memorized. He had practiced his 3-point turn, and the other maneuvers he would need to master. He had all the paperwork filled out and signed. He felt there was no question, he was ready. On the appointed day, Phillip strode into the Motor Vehicle office, and sat at one of the testing tables to take his exam along with all the other applicants scheduled for that day. It didn't take him long to finish the written portion of the test. Rules of the road, various road signs, and fundamental terminologies were pretty much child's play to Phillip, and he had no doubt that he had aced the written exam. Now, there remained only the road test. Phillip waited impatiently for his turn with the Motor Vehicle Officer. When it was time, he calmly opened the door and sat behind the wheel, buckling himself in and awaited instructions from the Officer. The road test was pretty much what Phillip had been expecting, and as the test concluded, the Officer told him he had passed. Phillip was ready to celebrate, but his mother wasn't ready to allow him to go driving around with his friends just yet. She wanted him to get a better feel of the road first. This would require taking all his aunts and uncles for a ride, as well as his older cousin.

It wasn't long before he had another visit from his Soulmate. He had been looking forward to his next encounter with her and was hoping that she might once again tell him how proud she was of him, acknowledging what he had accomplished as of late, but none of that happened. This time, it seemed she was more serious, and Phillip was wondering if a warning was coming. She did not smile but seemed to study him with those beautiful eyes of hers. She then said to him, "You must be prepared."

Then, the dream ended. Phillip lay in his bed feeling confused and frustrated.

"Why does she have to be so cryptic?" Phillip said to himself. "Can't she explain to me what she means a little more thoroughly?"

Whatever the meaning of her words, Phillip realized that he wasn't going to figure it out this night. He shrugged and went back to sleep. But it wasn't long before a new dream would manifest itself.

In this dream, he was driving down Route 313, a road which ran from Augusta to the coast, near Chambersburg and nearby coastal communities. It was late at night, and Phillip drove through a winding segment of a largely wilderness area, almost complete forest, with very few houses scattered along the way. He tempered his speed as he traveled this segment. There was always a chance that wildlife could emerge from the forest onto the road. One could encounter a deer, a moose, or even a bear, and this certainly would not be the best place for a collision with an animal. As the road neared the coast, Phillip would need to maneuver through a 3-point intersection with stop signs all around. It was a classic T-intersection except that upon approaching the intersection from Augusta, the road would split into two lanes with two different stop signs. If one was to take the right lane, it would mean a right turn at the stop sign and continuing to follow Route 313 for another six miles to Walnut Harbor. Phillip would be taking the left lane, meaning a left turn at the stop sign and following Beaver Brook Road for about three more miles of wilderness before seeing any houses as one approached the outskirts of Chambersburg. In his dream, Phillip approached the intersection, getting into the left lane in order to make a left turn at the stop sign. He sat at the stop sign for a moment, taking in the absolute darkness of the area. No houses, no lights, only the illumination of Phillip's headlights to show the way. He started to accelerate into the intersection but slammed on his brakes immediately. Something had caught his eye off to the left. He stared down Beaver Brook Road. A reflection of some sort? He couldn't be sure, but in an instant, another car, with its headlights off appeared out of nowhere, and ignoring its stop sign, flashed across the intersection right in front of Phillip's car. Phillip watched as the lightless car continued at a high rate of speed toward Walnut Harbor. Phillip realized there was no question that if he had not hit the brakes, the other car would have crashed into him.

This same dream kept repeating itself to Phillip for several months. Then, the unthinkable happened, or perhaps the predictable, depending on one's point of view. Phillip was traveling home at night from Augusta on Route 313. He was now traveling to Augusta once a week taking private lessons from the tuba player of the Augusta Symphony. The lessons had paid off, and Phillip had passed the audition for the Maine All-State Band two years in a row. However, on this night he had been delayed because he had stopped at one of the music stores in Augusta to pick up some music and a music stand light. As he approached the intersection that he had dreamed of so many times, he felt a bit nervous. Yes, it was only a dream, but who knew? He pulled up to the stop sign ready to make his left-hand turn. Following the protocol he learned in driving school, he waited at the stop sign and gazed to his left down Beaver Brook Road. Nothing. He glanced to his right. Nothing. As he was turning his head to look to his left again, Phillip watched, almost in shock, as a blue car, without headlights hurdled right in front of his car through the intersection. As the car passed in front Phillip's headlights, he could see into the car for a brief second. The car was full of teenage boys, some of them holding beer bottles. Phillip watched as the car flew out of sight. He began to shake.

"Did this really just happen?" he said to himself out loud.

He continued to sit at the stop sign, with no other cars in sight, trying to make sense of this encounter. The idea of a dream matching up with reality like this was astounding. Phillip realized that the reoccurring dream had prepared him to avoid what could have been a very serious accident. He thought of his Soulmate's words from months ago, "You must be prepared." He wondered if she had somehow been responsible for the reoccurring dream. If so, she may well have saved his life. Although still shaken, he finally felt ready to proceed. He gingerly eased his car into the intersection, and with a shudder, continued on his way home.

Chapter 8
Maybe She's Not Real

"Before you find your soulmate, you must first discover your soul." — Charles F. Glassman

Phillip never dreamed about the intersection again after his real life encounter. His Soulmate did not appear either and Phillip wondered about that. Could it be that she was losing interest in him? Was she starting to feel, as he did that a relationship carried on only through dreams wasn't very practical? Was it possible that while her wisdom was a big help to Phillip when he was growing up, but perhaps now, not as much anymore? Phillip didn't think so. He certainly could have used her insight the other day, when his mother sat Phillip and his brother down at the kitchen table and told them that she and their father were separating and would probably divorce. Phillip was shocked and felt powerless to deal with the situation. Even if his Soulmate could not offer any advice, a warning would have been helpful. Why was she not appearing?

Phillip could not come up with any answers, but one day in class, he was handed a note from Lydia. She was in a couple of his classes and sat behind him in home room period. Lydia looked very different from Phillip's Soulmate. She was a bit taller than his Soulmate, had light red hair and was of French-Canadian decent. He was aware of Lydia because it seemed that she was always trying to be near him and would try to find any reason to start a conversation with him. No matter what the class or event, if she could be there, she would. As Phillip read her note confessing her feelings for him, he realized he should be happy, and yet he wasn't. He had gone on a couple of casual dates with other girls, but with Lydia, based on the contents of her note, it seemed that dating her would be taking things to a new level. A feeling of guilt washed over him. Would dating Lydia be cheating on his Soulmate? In all the times his Soulmate appeared to him they never discussed it, but in Phillip's heart he believed that she was a real person.

Now he wondered if there was a connection with this issue and his Soulmate's long absence. Could it be that she decided it was time for Phillip to start thinking about carrying on relationships with real girls? Phillip spent a few days pondering this, but realized that after all, practicality had to win out. The next time he and Lydia met, it was awkward, but he asked her out. They continued to go out, many times ended up making out, but Phillip couldn't tell if this relationship was running its proper course. Was it typical of the relationships that other kids were having? At some point would he and Lydia arrive at "happily ever after"? Phillip didn't know the answers to these questions because he was never involved in a relationship before. It appeared that he had a long way to go before those answers came to light.

Chapter 9
Senior Year

"A soulmate is someone who has locks that fit our keys, and keys to fit our locks. When we feel safe enough to open the locks, our truest selves step out and we can be completely and honestly who we are; we can be loved for who we are and not for who we're pretending to be. Each unveils the best part of the other. No matter what else goes wrong around us, with that one person we're safe in our own paradise."

— Richard Bach

The only thing more exciting than beginning high school is the prospect of finishing high school. As Phillip, now age 18, entered the spring of his senior year in high school, he was aware of several experiences still awaiting him. In a last-minute decision, he and his brother decided to join the school Track and Field team. Not much of a runner, Phillip concentrated on the throwing events, the shot-put, javelin and discus. It felt strange being a Senior rookie on the team, and trying to master skills that many of his teammates had started learning when they were freshmen. He very much wanted to make a contribution to his team and earn a letter in track. To do this, he would have to score points in a track meet. However, he had to miss two track meets because of music. On the day of one meet, the school Spring Concert was scheduled in the evening, but after a long bus ride, Phillip would not have arrived back to the school in time for the concert and he had to prioritize. Music was going to be his field of study after high school, not track and field. There was also a track meet that he needed to miss on a Saturday, because he had an audition to become a music major at Franklin State

College. Phillip chose Franklin State because he knew it would be a financial strain on his family to send him to live on campus at the University of Maine, or in Portland. He could commute to Franklin State, which would make things more affordable.

As track season continued, Phillip was becoming frustrated. He realized that he was a rookie trying to master skills that the other athletes had spent years honing. Then, one night to his great joy, his Soulmate appeared to him. He knew he had a thousand questions for her, but he couldn't remember any of them. She gave him her usual adoring look and said, "Your answer is technique."

At first, Phillip was confused. Was she talking about music? Phillip decided that was doubtful. After all, he had pretty much nailed his Franklin State audition. Finally, he came to the conclusion that she was talking about the track team. It made sense, but at this point there were only three track meets left in the season, and Phillip had yet to score any points for his team. He had started wondering if he had made a mistake trying out for the team. He was no longer throwing the javelin. Even when he was in little league, Phillip realized that he had a poor throwing arm, and of the three events that he participated in, javelin was by far his weakest.

As the team bus arrived at St. George High School for today's meet, Phillip realized that if he was going to make any true contribution to his team, he needed to start now. The schedule of events for each meet was usually the same for the throwing events, shot-put, followed by discus, and finally, javelin. Phillip thought of his Soulmate's words and realized what he had to do. He would skip the shot-put event and use that time to work on his discus technique. While the shot-put competition was being held, Phillip spent his time over at the discus section of the field practicing his throws. Focusing on what his Soulmate had told him, he realized that the way to achieving maximum distance in his throw was to master his spin. Before releasing the discus, a thrower needed to complete a spin, one and a half times counterclockwise within the 2.5-meter throwing circle. While he was practicing, Phillip decided to use the college discus that for some reason had come into the team's possession. It was slightly thicker and weighed perhaps a couple of pounds more than a high school discus, which of course he would throw when he competed.

Phillip practiced throw after throw. It was hard to see if he was making any progress because when he used the college discus, his throws were usually about 20 feet less than with a normal high school discus. Eventually, the shop put event ended, and most of those involved headed over to the discus circle. Each contestant is allowed three throws in the competition. As Phillip entered the circle for his first throw, he was feeling confident. He went through his wind-up, completed his spin, and released the discus. Unfortunately, his body had little too much momentum, and in order to keep his balance he ended up stepping out of the circle.

"Foul!" the judge called.

It was a good throw, but it wouldn't count. Disappointed, Phillip took his place among the contestants. He watched the other contestants take their turns and kept replaying his previous throw in his mind. He watched as Danny, the best discus thrower on the team, take his turn. Danny made a good throw, 104 feet, but he wasn't happy with it, and felt he could do better. Finally, it was Phillip's turn again. He entered the circle with as much concentration as he could muster. And yet, he thought of his Soulmate. It almost seemed as if she was coaching him while he was awake. He grinned slightly, but quickly put it out of his mind. He started his wind-up, then his spin, and as soon as he released the discus he realized that this was one of those rare throws where everything clicked.

"Good throw Phil!" the assistant coach said.

Phillip smiled. He had made a few throws over a hundred feet, but this throw was farther than any other he had made. He held his breath as they measured the distance.

"One hundred thirteen feet, and five inches," the judge announced.

Phillip was exuberant. The extra work had paid off, and now it looked like he was going to score points for his team. He watched Danny take his second throw. Even though he and Danny got along ok, he knew that Danny would consider losing to Phillip to be unacceptable. However, as Danny released his discus, it seemed to leave his fingers prematurely. It was a good throw, but it landed a couple of feet outside of the foul line.

"Foul!" the judge called.

The St. George team had only one discus thrower who could only reach 89 feet, so there was no competition there. As the third round of throws began, Phillip realized that the only contestants that could beat his throw were Danny, and Bruce, a football lineman who was bigger and stronger than Phillip. When it was Phillip's third turn, he knew he wasn't going to make as good a throw as his previous one. As it turned out, his last throw went for 102 feet, but he still felt satisfied. He then watched Bruce take his final turn. Bruce didn't spend a lot of time mastering his spin. He relied mostly on his brute strength, and in this case, his throw went for 108 feet. The realization dawned on Phillip that he had a chance to win this event. As Danny took his final throw, Phillip held his breath. It was obvious that Danny was feeling the pressure, and he put as much effort into his throw as he possibly could. As he released the discus, Phillip realized that Danny was in trouble. He was suffering from the same issue that Phillip experienced on his first throw, too much body momentum. So much so, that Danny actually fell outside of the circle.

"Foul!" the judge called, and Phillip had a hard time believing what had taken place. As the judge read off the final results, with Phillip as the winner, he couldn't have been prouder. He smiled widely as Danny and Bruce congratulated him. Now, he really wondered what his Soulmate would say.

Senior year was almost over, but there were still things to experience. One of those was Senior Prom. When it came to the prom, Phillip's most fervent wish was that he could take his Soulmate as his date. What a magical night that could have been. Imagine being at such a wonderful event with literally the girl of your dreams.

Of course, it was obvious to Phillip that Lydia would be expecting him to ask her to the prom. He would comply, of course. After all, it was never a good idea to disappoint someone as the end of your high school days loomed. Besides, it wasn't as if there were an army of girls banging on his door wanting to go to the prom with him. Lydia was pretty, but nowhere near as much as his Soulmate. When they went to the prom, she wore a green gown that looked nice enough, but Phillip wasn't wild about the style. He told her she looked very nice anyway.

As Phillip walked across the stage to accept his diploma, he wasn't sure whether he was feeling pride or relief. He was certainly glad to be graduating, but there were surrounding circumstances that were bothering him. He had originally suggested to Lydia that they go to graduation together. She balked at that idea and told him she wanted to go with her family. Phillip's parents decided to go separately, since they were in the middle of their divorce. So, Phillip ended up driving to graduation by himself, and felt somewhat lonely driving home alone. There was something that was aggravating him about that. It seemed like throwing cold water on the celebration. Certainly, he had received an array of cards and graduation gifts from family members, and there would be a cake waiting for him when he got home, but for some reason it didn't seem like much of a celebration.

Chapter 10
More School Daze

"A strong soul reaches anyplace, anytime; body fails to restrain it. And thus, perhaps soulmates are formed."
— Munia Khan

Phillip's freshman year at Franklin State seemed to fly by, and for the most part, it was successful. He had aced his music theory class, which for freshmen music majors, was considered a critical class. He had held his own in most of his other classes, and the only disappointing grade he received was a 'D' in history. He was still seeing Lydia, but their relationship was not as smooth as he would have liked. He still felt comfortable being with her, but at times they seemed to argue over minor things. There were times when Phillip would consider asking Lydia out on a particular date, but then decide against it. It didn't seem like it was worth the possible aggravation. His Soulmate only appeared once to him during this time. He wanted to ask her why she had stayed away for so long. What was it that was holding her back from appearing to him, all of the questions that had been nagging at him regarding her decreased presence since his probable brush with death at that Route 313 intersection. But one look at her sitting there, in her unabashed beauty, and he couldn't bring himself to say anything. She, in turn, did not speak either, and the dream ended in silence.

Sophomore year was very different for Phillip than Freshman year. Some of his classes were less interesting, and some of his professors he simply did not care for. He struggled more in his piano class, his psychology class was a complete bore, and music theory, which he had breezed through his freshman year was now a class he struggled with. Not that he didn't want to learn the material, but the professor of the class was really substandard in his ability to get his students to relate to the material, and his teaching presentations were extremely dry. Needless to say, Phillip's fall semester grades took a big nosedive. Worse, a few days after his grades arrived, he received a letter from the Dean's office. The letter said that his grade point average had fallen below the minimum standard expected by the college. The minimum grade point average expected at colleges like Franklin State was 2.0, or basically a "C" average. Phillip's grade point average had fallen to 1.8, and he was now on academic probation. Phillip was taken aback by this, and all sorts of thoughts flooded his mind. Should he push on, and hope that things would get better? Should he change his major? And if so, to what? Phillip had no idea. Should he leave school altogether? After all, what was the point in staying if one couldn't be successful? What prospects would he then have. Go to work at a mill somewhere?

Then, one evening, to his relief and joy, he was visited by his Soulmate. He was half expecting to be berated by her for the miserable job he had been doing at school. The words never came. She sat there, on the wall, like she always did, as beautiful as ever, with her kind eyes non-verbally communicating to him that she was not upset. He started to smile, and she smiled back. She then said something that he was perhaps expecting but was nonetheless startled by it: "Why don't you try harder?"

After the dream ended, Phillip stared at his bedroom ceiling, like he so often did after her appearances.

"Why not try for A's?" he thought to himself.

It would be a considerable departure from Phillip's approach to school over the years. Even though he was very achievement oriented when it came to his other activities, Phillip generally held a disdain for school since he was in grade school. He was decidedly a "just get by" type of student.

"Just pass the class!" was a statement he would tell himself over and over. Most of the time it worked, sometimes it didn't.

"It certainly didn't work this past semester," Phillip murmured to himself. Perhaps a change in academic philosophy was warranted. The key word in all of this was "try." He didn't want to be a student fixated on always getting an 'A'. But the word "try."

"Even if I didn't get the 'A,' my grades would probably improve," Phillip thought. He turned over and went back to sleep armed with this new insight.

Chapter 11
The Turnaround

"A soulmate is the one person whose love is powerful enough to motivate you to meet your soul, to do the emotional work of self-discovery, of awakening." — Kenny Loggins

As the new semester began, Phillip was presented with the perfect way to test out his new academic approach. As part of his psychology requirement, Phillip had chosen the course "Personality Psychology." On the first day of class, the professor announced that everyone would decide what their grade in the course would be. For a 'C', there was a basic list of criteria that one would need to accomplish. For a 'B', a more extensive requirement list would have to be completed. In order to receive an 'A' one would need to complete all the requirements for a 'B', as well as an additional list of assignments and projects. Each student was given an academic contract designating which grade level they were going to attempt.

"Now, let the real test begin," Phillip thought as he circled the 'A' requirements on the form. A few days later, he received a visit from his Soulmate. Phillip was delighted that she appeared to him so soon after the last time.

She said to him, "Act confident."

Phillip wasn't sure what to make of it. He noted that she didn't say "Be confident." It was a bit perplexing.

Half the semester had passed. Phillip stood outside the studio about as nervous as he had ever been. The studio in question was actually the news booth at the college radio station. Phillip had joined the radio station, which was entirely staffed by students, at the beginning of the semester. Being on academic probation, he knew he wasn't supposed to join any clubs. But Phillip figured that as long as he didn't say anything to anyone, no one would make a fuss. He had gone through all the training, had gone to Boston to pass the exam for his third-class FCC license and was now cleared to start doing newscasts. He entered the news booth just before the top of the hour, put on the headphones and checked his news stories from the Associated Press news prompt one more time. He then thought of his Soulmate's words, "Act confident," and decided that now was as good a time as any to try it. When he heard newscast theme music, he came in with his cue exactly on time. That much, he knew he had down. After all, he had witnessed the opening of the college newscast dozens of times. As he started to read from his news stories, he was very aware of all of the radio station staff members gathering in the main studio, or in the hallway listening to him. Making a mistake in front of them would be bad enough. But the radio station was being piped into several offices on campus, the student union, campus cafeteria, and the community at large. A gas station down the street from the campus kept the radio station on its speaker system, and the station itself could be picked up as far away as Brookfield. Making a mistake for all of those people would be an embarrassment. With as confident a voice that he could muster, Phillip read through the national stories, state, and local news, and finally the weather forecast, which was provided by the Franklin State College Weather Station. Phillip gave the sign-off, and walked out of the news booth, to the congratulations and accolades of his fellow radio station members. During the newscast he hesitated a couple of times, but no major breakdowns. He was generally pleased with himself. He looked forward to his next newscast, which he hoped to do even better.

Unlike the first semester, the second semester seemed to fly by. In Phillip's psychology class, he thought he had completed all of the 'A' requirements, but his final grade was a 'B'. He didn't understand why he received the lower grade, but nonetheless he considered the experiment a success. Phillip thought "After all, if I had only done the minimum, I'd probably be looking at a 'D' or an 'F!'"

He was pleased that his new approach had brought similar results in the rest of his classes, and he could take pride in that he was no longer on the academic probation list.

However, his relationship with Lydia did not fare as well. Phillip was disturbed by what seemed to be a pattern of consternation whenever he would visit Lydia at her house. Most times, the consternation would stem from Lydia herself, who would treat him poorly in front of her family, or sometimes order him around. It was almost as if she had to show her family that she was in charge of the relationship, and it led to multiple arguments between he and Lydia when they were by themselves. Phillip hoped for an improvement in the situation, but it didn't seem to be happening. Finally, one day when he had come to visit, and as they sat at the table, Lydia's mother said to him, "You know, there are some job openings down at the foundry, and they pay pretty well. You should apply there. After all, if you're going to have a future with my daughter, you should have a good paying job, and while studying music is nice, being a music teacher isn't a real job."

Phillip rose from his chair. This was the proverbial "Last Straw."

Without saying a word, Phillip walked out of the house, with Lydia dashing behind him. His face was red with rage as he calmly and clearly told Lydia that he didn't want to see her again. He might rescind it later, but he kept that thought to himself. For the time being, anyway, their relationship would be on permanent hold. He turned, got into his car, and went for a long drive.

Chapter 12
The Final Semester

"The idea of a soulmate is beautiful and very romantic to talk about it in a movie or a song, but in reality, I find it scary." - Vanessa Paradis

Phillip looked at the course selection registration sheet in his hand. He stood in the middle of the gym floor as if he were an island unto himself among the wide-spread chaos throughout the rest of the gym as students rushed to sign up for spring semester courses. Phillip had spent the first semester of his senior year student teaching. He student-taught at a school with a very successful band program, conducting lessons and rehearsals under a very knowledgeable band director. Conducting a 125 piece band was quite daunting, but Phillip handled it well. He learned a lot, and he couldn't wait to apply that newfound knowledge to his own band program. Now, it was spring semester of his senior year, and it was time to finish up on whatever coursework he had yet to complete. At this point, he pretty much had all of his remaining course requirements lined up. The only thing he needed was one final elective course, and that would take care of all the requirements he would need for graduation. He continued to look through the course selection catalog, looking for just the right class to select. He didn't want to choose some mundane class that would bore him. He wanted something that would excite him. On the next to the last page of the course selection catalog, he found what he was looking for: Television Production. A course taught in the campus television studio that would familiarize students with all of the equipment and explore how television productions are put together. He wrote the class registration code on his registration sheet. Decision made. As he went to turn in his registration forms, he began to think of other topics. He checked his watch. He had ample time to make it back to Chambersburg to meet with his dad. For some reason, his thoughts turned to Lydia. It had been more than a year since he broke off his relationship with her. They had not had any contact since, although they would sometimes cross paths in public places. It had also been a similar amount of time since he had any contact with his Soulmate. He missed her terribly, but as always, he did not have the ability to contact her. He would have to wait until she appeared to him.

Phillip got out of his car and took a deep breath as he surveyed the landscape. The salt air of the ocean was as invigorating as ever, and a brisk January wind lashed the shoreline, the incoming tide showing an ominous presence displaying multiple whitecaps. In the distance, he could see several lights along the shore from various houses in the twilight. Although Phillip's relationship with his mother remained close, after his parents' divorce was final, Phillip saw very little of his father for the first couple of years. They would meet at Christmas, and once in a great while get together for some event, but their contact was minimal. However, in the last few months, his father, Jack, had purchased a cottage near Colony Beach and had it winterized so that he could stay there year-round. Today, Jack had invited Phillip to visit him in his new home, and Phillip decided to take advantage of the visit to have a long talk with his dad. At first, they engaged in small talk as Jack gave his son a tour of the cottage, but eventually, Phillip steered the conversation to what was weighing on his mind. He expressed his frustration with being unable to see his dad on a regular basis. He was afraid they would lose touch, and regardless of the divorce, he still wanted to be close to his father. At first, his father said nothing. They sat at the kitchen table and Jack stared at the ceiling as if he were struggling to find the right words.

"I need to apologize," he finally said. "I did not realize that things would turn out the way they did."

"I don't understand," said Phillip. "Why so little contact?"

"When your mother and I separated, I did not know what your reaction would be," replied Jack. "That's a conversation we should have had, and it's my fault that we didn't." Jack rested his elbows on the table. "I wanted to shield you from the animosity between your mother and I, and I was unsure of your feelings."

"I wasn't mad at you," Phillip replied.

"I realize that now," Jack explained, "but at the time, I didn't. I've read a lot about kids who ended up blaming themselves over their parents' divorce or blaming one of their parents and creating even more animosity as a result. I didn't want to see anything like that happen." He smiled slightly.

"Plus, there's a reason I didn't want to make any demands on your time." Phillip had a quizzical look as his father continued. "I've never told you this, and I don't think you're aware, but after high school, I spent a year attending college in Rhode Island."

"You did?" Phillip said. "No, I wasn't aware, I thought you went into the Army."

"I did," replied his dad, "but that was after my failed stint as a college student. My father had high hopes for me, and I felt that I had let him down."

"Did he tell you that?" Phillip asked.

"He didn't have to," Jack replied, "but my college experience taught me how difficult it can be to achieve success there. You know, our family goes back to colonial times, and we have a history of being farmers until the industrial revolution when we switched to factory jobs." Jack's face broke out in a full smile. "And now, look at you, a college senior, and when you graduate this spring, you'll be the first member of this family to be a college graduate in at least several generations, perhaps ever."

Phillip smiled. "I never thought of that," he said.

"Well," Jack replied, "I don't know if we can make up for lost time, but I certainly think we can make the most of the present."

Chapter 13
She Finally Appears (Well, Maybe)

"What are the chances you'd ever meet someone like that? Someone you could love forever someone who would forever love you back? And what did you do when that person was born half a world away?" — Rainbow Rowell

Classes started about a week later, and on the appointed day, Phillip went to his first Television Production class. He walked into the television studio and stopped in his tracks. There, seated in the middle of the group of students was a Chinese girl. She had straight black hair that extended to just below her shoulders, and her forehead was covered with bangs. Her height and build seemed to match his Soulmate as well. He wasn't sure if her facial features exactly matched, but she was pretty darn close. She did not wear a white dress like his Soulmate but wore long pants and a red sweater. After all, it was January in Maine. He found an open seat right next to her and decided that he immediately needed to start a conversation with her. He looked at her and smiled. This would be the first time in his memory that he ever spoke to a girl he just met. With as big a smile as he could muster, he said, "Hi, my name is Phillip."

She smiled nervously at him and said, "I am Eliza."

Phillip thought to himself, "Well, that's good. She didn't run out of the room screaming, so it's a start."

He continued to ask her questions. What was her major?

"I study business," she replied.

At this point, he noticed that her English had some flaws, mostly with pronunciation. It was probably safe to ask her his next question. "Where are you from?" he asked.

This time, her smile was more genuine as she replied, "I am from Hong Kong."

Phillip started to explain where he was from and what he was studying when the professor called the class to order. To Phillip, the professor looked to be in her early thirties. He wondered how she could have gotten the background to teach this class, but when she started talking about the various equipment in the studio, and how the production techniques would be utilized; her knowledge of the subject was obvious. The first few classes revolved around the basics, equipment operation, production terminology and the like.

While he tried not to be too obvious, Phillip kept his eye on Eliza as much as he could. Whether or not she was his Soulmate personified was a question yet to be answered, but there was no question she was just as beautiful. He would try to engage her in conversation before each class. She would not talk about herself a whole lot, although he was able to get her to talk about her aspirations in the business world when she finished her education. After the first couple of weeks, the class started to produce small video segments. For each segment, the roles of the students would change. Phillip did well with all of his roles operating studio equipment. He did get tripped up though when he was operating one of the two cameras. Operation of the cameras seemed simple enough, but some of the camera shots that Phillip framed were out of focus. Eliza also encountered difficulties in doing voice-over announcing as her struggle to master English surfaced. Phillip tried to encourage her, and she seemed to appreciate that. While Phillip appreciated the cordial relationship he had developed with Eliza, he felt somewhat frustrated that he could not get her to talk about herself. Moreover, he sensed that he had to be very careful if he were to guide their relationship beyond cordial. What he really wanted to do was grab her by the shoulders, look directly into those beautiful eyes and ask her if she had ever dreamed about him. Imagine what would happen if she were to answer "yes." But, alas, he realized that was something he could not do. Phillip may have been inexperienced with girls, but he wasn't stupid. She would probably think that he was totally nuts, and their fragile relationship would be ruined.

A few weeks later, the professor announced the next assignment for the class. She called it the commercial project, and everyone would have to write, produce, and direct their own commercial. When each person's turn came, they would have to dole out assignments to every member of the class, pass out scripts and cue sheets, and take the director's place in the control room. Phillip devised a commercial that involved a Martian who had just arrived on earth and was very hungry from the trip. The earthling that he encounters runs a store and tells him that what he needs is a travel guide, which is the product featured in the commercial. The earthling then recites a litany of the features of the travel guide, including its restaurant listings. In a humorous twist at the end, Phillip arranged for the camera focus on a full screen shot of the travel guide on display next to the human to finish the commercial. The last two lines are heard during that final shot, in the background, as the earthling asks the Martian, "Can I wrap it for you?"

And the Martian replies, "No thanks, I'll eat it here!"

The professor called Phillip's commercial "Wonderfully creative" and asked everyone if they would be willing to do an additional take.

"Incredible!" thought Phillip.

This could be significant. It may well indicate that she may want a copy of his commercial to show to future classes. As everyone prepared for the next take, Phillip spotted Eliza over in the corner of the control room. Her assignment was the sound board, and she was poking through a box looking for a microphone cord. Phillip walked over to her, and she looked up and smiled at him. There it was. The same smile he had seen on his Soulmate countless times. The smile he had dreamed of since he was a little boy. Phillip immediately had an uncontrollable impulse to grab her hands, confess to her that she was the girl of his dreams and profess his love for her.

He started to move his arms to take hold of her hands. He didn't know what he would say to her, but his feelings were overwhelming, and at the bursting point. His actions were interrupted when he heard his name being called. It was the student running the character generator. Apparently, there was a question about one of the graphics. Phillip sighed and walked over to the character generator to see what the matter was. Afterward, Phillip promised himself that at some point he would sit down with Eliza and tell her his story.

Phillip and Jack agreed that they would meet once a week, on Tuesdays, for dinner. Sometimes they would just order a pizza, but depending on the time of low tide, Jack would arrange to come home from work early, grab his old sneakers, his pitchfork and a pail, and head out to the sandbars to dig for clams. By the time Phillip arrived at the cottage, there would be a bowl of steaming clams ready for them. Phillip treasured these weekly dinners, but on this particular evening, he seemed pre-occupied. Jack noticed it as well.

"Is something wrong son?" he asked.

Phillip didn't answer at first. He sighed, sat back in his chair, and said, "I'm not sure."

He went on to tell his father about Eliza, although he never mentioned her resemblance to his Soulmate. In fact, he never told his father about his Soulmate, nor anyone else for that matter. He did confess that he had strong feelings for her, and finally said, "I'm just having a hard time getting her to open up to me. She never talks about anything personal during our conversations."

Now it was Jack's turn to sit back in his chair and sigh. He hadn't given Phillip any advice since Phillip was 10 and playing Little League baseball.

"You know," he began, "My father once told me when I was in college, that he thought most girls on campus were simply looking for a husband."

Jack was amused by Phillip's frown.

"I never really believed that," he continued. "And I certainly would not expect it to be true today, but I just don't know what this girl's cultural norms are in her part of the world. I'm not sure if you're interested in advice from your old man, but it seems to me that you need to focus on why she never mentions anything personal. It could be just a cultural thing for her, but there could be a real reason behind it. You should speak to her about it."

"Not a conversation I'd be looking forward to," grumbled Phillip.

"Give it some thought," his father replied, "I'm sure you can be diplomatic about it."

As the semester ran its course, Phillip remained discouraged by the lack of progress he was making with Eliza in cultivating their relationship. Remembering his father's advice, he decided he needed to observe her from a distance outside of class. Nothing overt, just seeing if there was a possibility that he might see some facet of her personality that she might exhibit outside of the classroom. He spent extra time in the student center and the library. He only ran into her a couple of times. Each time, they would smile and say "hi" and continue on their ways.

One day, Phillip was sitting in a booth in the library lounge, enjoying a soft drink and pastry. The lounge was located along a busy corridor between sections of the library. It was dotted with tables and chairs, a couple of booths, and an array of vending machines. The booths were a little more isolated than the tables, so when Eliza walked through the area with a couple of friends, she didn't notice Phillip sitting off to the side. Eliza and her friends were being trailed by a half dozen or so boys. Everyone appeared to be Chinese, and they were speaking to each other in what Phillip assumed was Chinese. Some of the boys appeared to be flirting with Eliza, and she appeared to be flirting back. As she bantered back and forth with the boys, Phillip took note of her facial expression and mannerisms. This was a side of her that he had never seen in class.

"Realization stings," Phillip muttered to himself.

It certainly appeared that the friendliness she showed him in class could simply be a friendliness she would show anyone in a foreign land. Phillip envied those boys. Wouldn't it have been wonderful if she could let down her guard with him the way she did with them. As the group travelled through to the next section of the library, Phillip pondered his situation. With doubt creeping in, it now seemed that cultivating the relationship that he desired with Eliza now seemed more complicated. He realized that it was imperative that he sit down with Eliza and talk with her. But it was very clear that even if he did, there was no guarantee of success.

Before Phillip knew it, it was the final week of the semester. Only two more class days remained for the television production class. On Monday, Phillip arrived at class early. He wanted to have a clear opportunity to speak with Eliza. But for some reason, Eliza was not in class that day. Phillip thought that was odd. This class was the last chance to pull together any last random material issues. Wednesday's class, the final class, would be devoted to taking the final exam. Phillip made some extra trips to the library and student center in hopes of bumping into Eliza, but to no avail. As Wednesday's class started, Phillip asked the professor about Eliza since she was absent again.

"Well, Eliza asked me if she could take her exam last week," said the professor. "Apparently she needed to leave campus early."

Phillip was devastated. He struggled to take the exam, fighting back tears the whole time. When he finished his exam, he handed it in to the professor, bade her farewell, and walked to his car. He sat behind the wheel but did not start the engine. He just stared at the dashboard for a very long time. "She's gone." he kept repeating to himself. He didn't know where she went, how to contact her. He remembered asking her a couple of weeks ago what her plans were once the semester ended. She said she didn't know. Phillip now wondered if that was true. He had been waiting for the perfect opportunity to talk with her, but the perfect opportunity never materialized. He now realized he could have made an opportunity but didn't.

"I hereby pronounce you Phillip the Chicken," he said to himself out loud. "I wonder if telling her my story would have made a difference?"

Now he would never know. The only thing he did know was that this was a failure that would nag him the rest of his life.

Chapter 14
Lydia Returns

"The Buddhists say that if you meet somebody and your heart pounds, your hands shake, and your knees go weak, that's not the one. When you meet your Soulmate you'll feel calm. No anxiety, no agitation. – Monica Drake

The next evening, Phillip was sitting in the family kitchen studying. His last final exam, Spanish, was scheduled for the next day. He was one of those students that just didn't find it easy to study a foreign language. He certainly knew he wasn't going to get an 'A' in this class, but he sure as hell wanted to make sure he didn't flunk. To work for four years passing courses of all kinds, and then flunking the last final exam before graduation was certainly not something Phillip wanted to experience. He was studying future tense, something he was sure would be on the exam when he heard someone knocking at the back door. His mother was out shopping, and his brother was out with friends. As far as he knew, no one was expected to stop by. He opened the door, and there stood Lydia, looking very apprehensive. She said, "I need to talk with you."

Phillip nodded and invited her in. She took a seat at the kitchen table next to his. She looked at him for a few seconds before saying anything. Phillip noticed that her eyes appeared tear streaked.

"I wanted to say I'm sorry about how things turned out between us," she began. "I've thought about it a lot, and there were some things I said, some things I did, that I probably shouldn't have. What I'm trying to say is I would really like us to resume our relationship, start over, I guess. The thing is,

I can't bear to lose you forever. You're going to be graduating and taking a job God knows where."

She got that part right anyway Phillip thought. He had sent applications for teaching positions to schools in all of the New England states, New York State, and New Jersey. He had also heard that Lydia had graduated nursing school a few months ago and had taken a job at a local nursing home. Phillip thought about it for a few moments. Since they broke up, Phillip had gone on a couple of dates with other girls, but they led nowhere. He was also still very upset over losing Elisa.

"I don't know if this will go anywhere," he thought to himself, "but I suppose there's no harm in giving it another shot." Wordlessly, he reached out to hug her, and she fell into his arms.

After Phillip's graduation, he saw Lydia on a frequent basis. They grew closer as the summer went on. When Phillip was invited to interview for the Band Director position at Stony Lake High School, on the edge of Maine's White Mountains, he asked Lydia if she wanted to go with him, sort of as a good luck charm. She agreed, and while Phillip met with the school administrators, Lydia took his car to explore the town. As summer ended, Phillip wasn't sure where their relationship would end up, but he had to admit he was open to anything.

Chapter 15
Seven Years Later

"My eyes saw you, but damn, did my soul feel you."—
Melody Lee

He looked at her sadly, as if he knew something he wasn't supposed to. But her usual smile had its usual effect, and he couldn't help but smile back. He gazed at her for a long time, as if a thousand unspoken messages were being exchanged between them. They then both laughed at something neither said. Phillip had the feeling that it was the last thing they would ever share.

He awoke with a start. A familiar feeling of euphoria washing over him, the ultimate feeling of contentment.

"Wow!" Phillip thought, "I've really missed that feeling."

It had been several years since his Soulmate had visited him. He had forgotten about how he would feel in the aftermath of each visit. He felt a stirring near his legs on the bed. It was his son, Nickolas, now almost three, turning in his sleep. Lydia must have brought him to their bed sometime during the night. Nick was experiencing his own bout with night terrors. Perhaps it was the dancing lights, or maybe something else, but it seemed the only way he could sleep through the night was in his parents' bed. He glanced over at his wife. Lydia appeared to be sleeping soundly as well. Marriage to her wasn't easy, but they were managing. There were times when Phillip would catch himself making comparisons between Lydia and his Soulmate. Each time he would try to put it out of his mind. After all, it just wasn't fair to Lydia.

He glanced out the bedroom window, twilight was just starting to break. The painted leaves outside were waving back and forth in an early October breeze. It was just about time to get ready for school. His lesson plan today would be fairly simple, finish polishing the band's presentation for their performance at the Stony Lake High School football game on Saturday. Phillip sat on the bed and turned on the light. He glanced at his watch, the digital one that Lydia had made him go out and buy. Before they were married, Phillip tended to stay at school and work into the evening, his car usually being the last one to leave the faculty parking lot. Nowadays, the alarm on his watch would sound in the afternoon at 4:30pm. Lydia insisted that when the alarm sounded, he would drop whatever he was doing at school and head home.

Phillip sighed as he stared at the ceiling. He had a hard time believing this may have been the last visit from his Soulmate. He hoped he was wrong, but he had been waiting for this visit from her for so long. There were so many times when he would shut his eyes at night and will her to appear, as if commanding his unconscious self to make it happen, but to no avail. It was kind of ironic that no words were exchanged during this visit. No advice. No insights.

"Maybe she thinks I'm doing everything correctly," Phillip thought as he got up to start dressing. His thoughts turned to Eliza. How sad it was that he could never truly connect with her. He wondered what had happened to her. He had googled her name a couple of times, but it turned up nothing. He wondered where she was. Was she happy? Certainly, Phillip would unconditionally be willing to acknowledge that he loved his wife, but as the years went by, every now and then, perhaps more times than he would readily admit, Phillip would think of his Soulmate and ask himself, "What if?"

(End)

Whitecaps of Evergreen Lake

Chapter 1
The Field Trip

The water was slightly wavy in the mild breeze, but still quite pleasant. The tiny ripples made a welcoming sound as they lapped upon the beach, a clear invitation to anyone hearing it to go for a swim. As he stood on the edge of the beach, Evan knew that on this particular day, swimming was not on the agenda. After all, it was late May, and even though the weather had warmed up and clearly suggested short sleeves in the warmth of the afternoon, chances were the water was still quite chilly. Besides, he was on chaperone duty. The prospect of entering the cold water didn't stop some of the students from changing into their bathing suits before leaving the school on their field trip. Evan's gaze traveled across the beach watching the 5th grade students carefully. Yesterday, he had sat in on Brad's class as the 5th grade classroom teacher laid down the rules for the field trip. Students could walk into the water up to their waist, but no further. Evan now recalled Brad's words as some of the students were taking that rule to the limit.

Evan and Brad had been friends since they had both started teaching at the local elementary school six years earlier. After their first couple of years, when Brad came up with the idea of a field trip. This was the fourth year that they were chaperoning this trip together. As Brad's assistant chaperone he would have to be on guard for any infractions. Breaking the rule would mean spending the rest of the afternoon sitting on the bus. Some students stood off to the side by the picnic tables, not wanting to go into the water. Evan understood, this activity wasn't everybody's cup of tea. The rest of the students waded through the shallows, some ankle deep, some knee deep. Many of them carried kitchen strainers which they regularly dipped into the water in an effort to catch some of the small aquatic creatures that tended to stay in shallow water. Some of them captured small fish, tiny fry that hopefully would develop into adult perch or bass at some point. Others captured extremely small fish, known locally as pinheads. They were really small, only a few millimeters long, with oversized eyes, and translucent bodies. A couple of girls also found some freshwater clams. Suddenly Evan heard Brad's name being called.

"Mr. Davis! Mr. Davis!" he heard as two boys came running up to Brad.

"Look what we found!" Adam exclaimed as he and Ryan showed him their catch, a small, brown, crustacean.

"Good job boys!" Brad told them. "Do you know what it is?"

"A crayfish," Adam answered.

"No, a crawfish," Ryan argued.

"Both names are acceptable," Brad answered. He then continued with his impromptu quiz "Do you know what it eats?"

"It's a scavenger!" said Ryan.

"Yeah! it eats dead fish and plants," added Adam.

"Essentially correct," Brad replied, "excellent."

Evan checked his watch, then walked over to Brad, and showed it to him. Brad nodded and blew his whistle. The students stopped what they were doing and turned their attention to him. "Okay everybody," Brad announced. "It's time to head back to the school. Everyone release whatever you have caught back into the water and head for the bus."

Collective groans rose from the students as they carried out his instructions. The group of students that had spent their time at the picnic tables moved toward the water as their friends emerged from the shallows.

"Okay, Margo-Sub," Brad said quietly to Evan, "let's go."

Evan ignored the comment. Its origin harkened back to a time before the field trips started. When Evan and Brad started teaching at Lakeport Elementary School. The fourth grade teacher, Margo Bernier taught in the room next door to Brad. The three became fast friends during their first year teaching together. Both Evan and Brad were astounded at Margo's beauty. A former Miss Maine, it seemed to Evan that she evoked a positive effect on everyone she encountered. Many mornings, before school started, Evan would sit in the school cafeteria with his morning cup of coffee, and watch the students and staff enter the building. When Margo would walk through the door, it was as if she lit up the place. In Evan's case, he would always be faithful to his wife, Mya, and when he noticed that Brad and Margo were becoming quite close and was happy for both of them. As the three of them sat together at the faculty lunch on the last day of school in June, Brad outlined his idea for a field trip to Evergreen Lake to both of them.

"I think that sounds wonderful," said Margo. "You should absolutely approach the administration with this."

"I agree," added Evan.

Brad laughed and turned to Margo. "Would you like to be my assistant chaperone?"

"Certainly," she replied. "In fact, once I see how the first year goes, I may want to bring my class along as well."

"Excellent," said Brad.

The three continued to talk, and Evan was also able to get Margo to agree to sing a solo at the next school Christmas concert. All three left school that day looking forward to the following school year. However, tragedy struck one month later, when Margo was killed in a car accident. The following September, Brad pitched his field trip idea to the administration almost as a tribute to Margo, and asked Evan to be his assistant chaperone. "You mean I'm your Margo substitute?" he asked half-jokingly.

"Something like that," Brad replied. "I hereby pronounce you my 'Margo-sub.'"

They would refer to the term from time to time over the years, although Evan knew better than to open a discussion of those days.

As Brad and the students started walking toward the parking lot, Evan glanced across the cove, his eyes focusing on the Buker cottage. He was startled as he noticed what appeared to be a figure standing on the front deck, looking out over the water.

"Could it be?" Evan thought to himself. "She didn't say anything to me about coming. It certainly couldn't be anyone else, and yet, it's been years!"

Evan followed Brad and the students on to the bus. He took attendance, just to be sure, and the bus headed back to the school.

Chapter 2
She Makes Contact

The classrooms of Lakeport Elementary School were alive with the hustle and bustle of students preparing to go home at the end of the school day. As Evan and Brad entered the 5th grade classroom, they watched over the students as they cleared their desks and stuffed their backpacks. After all of them had left, the duo headed for the main office. After greeting the secretaries at the main desk, they walked over to the open doorway marked "Principal" and stood in the doorway. Mike was sitting at his desk working on his computer.

"Hi Mike," Brad said. "Just checking in. The trip went fine."

"I know," replied Mike, "Mrs. Branch had to speak with some of the students for making too much noise when they entered the building."

"Oh, sorry about that," Evan said.

"It's not a problem," Mike reassured them. "They were just excited coming back from the trip. However, the next time, I might suggest that you keep them in a group as they get off the bus and walk them into the building together. It's easier to monitor them that way."

Evan returned to the music classroom, logged on to his computer, and pulled up his set of lesson plans for the next day to make final adjustments. About fifteen minutes later, just at about the time that the lesson plans were finished, the teacher dismissal bell rang. Evan really didn't care for the idea of having to wait for a bell to ring before being able to leave the school for the day. To him, it was demeaning, as if the teachers could not be trusted to perform their duties properly. However, it appears that someone, perhaps the superintendent, or maybe a school board member felt a need to verify that teachers were putting in the required amount of time in the school building before heading home. With a sigh, Evan walked out to the parking lot and got into his car. Before he could start the car, his cell phone went off. He checked the caller ID. It was the call he was expecting.

He activated the call and said, "Hi Amy."

"Hello Evan," his stepmother replied. "I'm at the cottage, and if you're free, I was wondering if you could stop by."

"I'm just leaving school now," said Evan, "I'll see you in a little bit."

He started the car and drove off. The radio in the car was tuned to a late afternoon news program. Announcers were covering a breaking story regarding the state budget, including interviews with leading state legislators and the Governor. It seems there was a shortfall in state revenues and the politicians were now scrambling to adjust the state budget with only days left before the legislative session ended for the year. Like many other states, the State of Maine, by statute, had to approve a balanced state budget, without any shortfalls. As a result, the newly discovered revenue shortfall meant that the legislators and Governor needed to pass an adjusted budget reflecting the new revenue numbers. Evan turned off the radio. It seemed this was much ado about nothing. Besides, the budget for the Lakeport School District had been approved at the annual Town Meeting two months earlier.

With the radio turned off, Evan turned his thoughts to Buker cottage and his stepmother, Amy. Evan had lost his mother to breast cancer when he was eight years old. For five years after his mother had passed, his father, Carlton, who hadn't dated nor shown any interest in other women met Amy on a crowded San Francisco cable car. The two began a relationship, and about a year later they married. Each continued in their careers, Carlton as a lawyer in one of San Francisco's top law firms, and Amy as a reporter at the San Francisco Sentinel. Amy had spent her summers growing up on Evergreen Lake.

Her parents, Gordon and Marjorie Buker lived just outside of Boston, and purchased the cottage when Amy was quite young.

"I don't understand. Why is she here?" Evan thought to himself as he approached Evergreen Lake.

Chapter 3
The Reunion

Evan put on his turn signal as he approached the dirt road. As he turned into the road, he took note of the sign listing the property owners, Sacher, Greene, Morrill, Slater, Jobe, and finally, Buker. The first five hundred feet or so of the dirt road was at one time an old logging road. The road then split, with the old logging road continuing off to the right, while the left fork led to the cabins and cottages of the afore-mentioned owners. The road ran parallel to the lakefront, passing each lakefront property along the way. The final property at the end of the road was Buker Cottage. Evan pulled his vehicle up behind a blue sedan with Massachusetts plates, obviously a rental car out of Boston.

He got out of his car and walked onto the deck on the lakefront side of the cottage. It was a spectacular view, looking across the water to the other side of the lake, and the mountains beyond. Evan had always marveled at this view, especially when the leaves turned in the fall.

Putting the memory aside, Evan knocked on the door. After a few seconds, Amy opened the door, and greeted Evan with a warm smile. Evan hugged her and gave her a kiss on the cheek.

"How have you been?" Evan asked.

"Oh, I'm doing ok," Amy replied.

To Evan, Amy looked more than ok, with soft brown hair that framed a youthful face, showing very little in the way of age lines, and not even a single gray hair. Although she was nearly 60, Evan guessed she could probably pass for a woman in her 40's.

"How are Mya and the kids?" she asked.

"They're fine," Evan replied. "Isabel turned three last month, and Jeffery will enter 1st grade in the fall."

"Wow!" Amy said. "They certainly grow up fast."

"Indeed, they do," Evan replied.

His eyes started a sweep around the cottage interior as he had done hundreds of times, almost as if he needed to make sure nothing was out of place. The interior was mostly one large room with a small kitchen area off to the side and a large sitting area taking up the rest of the room.

Toward the back of the room were two doorways with the doors ajar. One of the doorways led to a bathroom while the other, a bedroom. Off to the left was a steep looking set of stairs that led to a loft where there were two more bedrooms. His gaze fell upon the wall opposite the kitchen area, known as the Archive Wall. The wall contained a lot of memorabilia from Gordon and Marjorie's careers. Several awards for Marjorie including a couple of "Teacher of the Year" awards from the school district she taught in, as well as a yearbook dedication the final year before her retirement. There were several of Amy's ribbons that she had won at the Evergreen Lake annual swim meet in her teenage days. For Gordon's part, there was a photo of the Boston University Math Department as well as a citation from the Dean. Also framed on the wall, was Gordon's retirement announcement in the Boston University student newspaper.

"Refresh my memory," he said to her, "when did your folks purchase this place?"

Amy thought for a moment and said, "I think I was maybe five or six then. Why do you ask?"

"I know you told me once," Evan replied, "but I couldn't remember. You know, when I first started coming here, this place grew on me exponentially, and yet, you seem to have kept your distance over the last several years. Has being a 'Big City Editor' cut into your time that much?"

Amy chuckled, "To an extent I guess," she replied.

After a moment, she grew serious. "Not all of my memories here were pleasant. My father was a relentless task master at times. He was very achievement oriented and believed that a person should always be working to achieve something." She pointed to the archive wall. "Those ribbons you see? A lot of blood, sweat and tears went into them."

"He was never that way with me," Evan pointed out.

"Which supports my theory that he really wanted a son instead of a daughter," she responded.

Evan thought for a moment. "Is that why you decided to go to Stanford?" he asked.

"My mother was very upset when I decided to go there. My father? Not so much. As I think about those years, it almost feels like child abuse."

"I can't imagine what that was like," replied Evan. "Perhaps he mellowed a bit by the time he met me."

"Perhaps," she responded. "They certainly went all out for you when you decided to enroll at Berklee."

In fact, when Gordon and Marjorie found out that Evan planned to attend the Berklee College of Music, they practically insisted that Evan stay with them in their home near Boston. That way, Evan would be spared the expense of room and board at the college. Each summer, he would stay with them at Buker Cottage while earning money for school at a local ice cream stand.

After a few moments, Evan asked, "Were you upset at the way your parents treated me?"

Amy was quick to respond, "Absolutely not, in fact it was kind of fun watching you experience new things. You had never been in a motorboat before. You loved the bicycle boat, and watching you struggle to learn how to steer the canoe was, well, let's just say that was 'interesting.'"

"You don't have to sugar coat it," said Evan. "I know I was awful at first."

Amy laughed. "Do you remember that you had never gone fishing until my father took you?" she said.

"How can I forget?" Evan responded. "That was the day he caught his prize bass," he said as he pointed to the archive wall.

Mounted there was Gordon's proudest achievement, a largemouth bass, 14 inches long that Gordon had sent to the local taxidermist to be mounted and hung on the wall. Evan remembered that day with crystal clarity. A couple of days after Evan and Carlton had been introduced to her parents, Amy and Carlton set out on a trip to Bar Harbor. They asked Amy's parents if they would look after Evan while they were gone. Marjorie immediately agreed, although Gordon seemed less than enthusiastic about babysitting young Evan. He decided to take Evan fishing and was amused to find out that this would be a brand-new experience for Evan, having never gone fishing before. Gordon showed Evan how to put on a life preserver, and they set off in the family motorboat. Upon arriving at Gordon's favorite spot, he showed Evan how to bait a fishing hook, and how to cast. It wasn't long before Evan hooked his first fish, a small perch. A bit later, Gordon's rod went wild, and after much effort, he ended up pulling in the biggest largemouth bass he had ever caught.

"I had a feeling," Gordon said as he secured his prize catch. "I found a penny on the floor when I woke up this morning."

"A Penny?" Evan said sounding confused.

"That's right," replied Gordon. "You see, my father always believed that when you found a penny, that a departed family member was looking after you. My father and I used to spend a lot of time fishing together. So, when I found the penny this morning, I couldn't help but think that he was watching over me."

Evan had never heard of this before, but as he examined the bass, he realized he couldn't argue with the result.

Amy's voice brought Evan back to the present. "Evan," she said, "there's something I need to tell you."

Evan sat down in the rocker. "I figured you were here for a reason. What is it?"

After a slight hesitation, Amy replied in a quiet voice, "It's time for me to sell the cottage."

Chapter 4
Some Frank Discussion

Evan's jaw dropped. "You can't be serious!"

"I'm afraid I am," Amy replied.

"Why?"

"Well, the major reason is the situation with your dad."

Evan's eyes grew wide. "Oh hell," he said, "I'm so embarrassed, I forgot to ask. How is he doing?"

"His condition hasn't changed much since your visit in January."

"I still don't understand," said Evan. "How did they miss the brain bleed? Didn't they bother asking him if he hit his head in the crash?"

"I haven't been able to get any satisfactory answers," she replied. "I don't even know if they checked for bleeding until he had the stroke."

Evan thought for a moment. "Has he responded at all to the therapy sessions?" he asked.

"Very minutely. It looks like it's going to take a long time for him to recover, if he recovers at all." After a few seconds, Amy continued, "Things are still in a state of flux. I've been holding meetings with Carlton's accountant as well as an elder attorney from his firm. Your father planned to roll his IRA into a different retirement account when he was ready to retire. Now, it's very complicated. There is the question of how to handle his IRA now that it looks like he may be a resident of the nursing home for a long time. It will most likely be necessary to file papers to change his IRA status to hardship distribution, but officially for now, he is still the senior partner at the firm. Everything is moving very slowly. The accountant and the elder attorney can't seem to agree on a unified strategy, and I don't really have the knowledge to make these decisions on my own. We've gone through a significant amount of our savings keeping him in the nursing home, and I need to start examining other financial options."

Evan stared at the floor. Amy kept going, "I know this place means a lot to you, and through the years, I've had no problem with you staying here each summer. Especially after dad died, I know mom treasured you being here with her in the summertime."

"I appreciate that," Evan interrupted. "But it's more than just about me these days. I wanted to see my children grow up here. Jeffery is now big enough to reach the pedals on the bicycle boat. I gave him a child's fishing rod for Christmas and promised to take him fishing this summer. Izzy is old enough now that I think she can appreciate playing in the water and the beach sand. Couldn't I just purchase the cottage from you?"

"I don't think you can afford it," Amy replied. "I spoke to Matt Hamel at the real estate office in town. He thinks this cottage could sell for as much as $ 350,000."

More silence as Evan tried to absorb what was happening.

"You're right," he said. "I could never afford that."

"Besides," Amy added, "the taxes on the property went up this year and the tax bill was $2200. The front deck is 30 years old and needs extensive repairs if not total replacement. And the roof isn't far behind."

"Well, that's not my fault," Evan argued. "You haven't been here since your mother's funeral, which was what...seven? eight years ago? I mean, I've done some minor repairs around here during that time, but you've basically been an absentee owner since then."

"I'm not going to argue over whose fault it is," Amy replied. "When your father became senior partner, and I was promoted to city editor at the Sentinel, it became very difficult for us to find the time to come here. Besides, you've been spending your summers here since you were in college, and I assumed the place was in good hands."

At that point, Evan's cell phone started ringing. He checked the caller ID. "Oh hell," he exclaimed. "She's probably wondering where I am."

He activated the call from his wife. "Hi Mya...No, I'm sorry, I lost track of time...I'm over at the cottage. Amy's here...Yes, I'm heading out now. I'll see you in a little bit...Bye."

He hung up the phone and said to Amy, "I have to get going. Can we continue this discussion? Maybe tomorrow?"

"Sure," Amy replied. "I'm staying here until Monday, then I'm heading home."

"I'll give you a call tomorrow," Evan said as he walked out the door.

As Evan gazed across the water from the deck, he was overwhelmed with sadness. He thought of all the happy memories he had accumulated over the years here. He looked down at the water's edge where the waves washed against the small beach and swimming area. Just last summer, he and Jeffery spent the afternoon together building a rudimentary sandcastle there. His gaze shifted off to the left, where the new aluminum dock sat.

It had been Evan's contribution to the cottage, replacing the old wooden dock, which was in very bad shape after being battered by spring ice floes over many years. The new aluminum dock had the advantage of easily being moved into the water at the start of the season and being moved back on to land for the winter. Next to the dock sat the canoe, the bicycle boat, and the motorboat, all under their winter coverings awaiting a new season of use. Evan remembered fondly his second year at Buker Cottage when Gordon had allowed him to take the motorboat out by himself for the first time. The experience of cruising across the open water at top speed was nothing short of exhilarating for teenager Evan. And now, each evening, just before dusk, the lake would become very placid, with a mirror-like surface across the water. It was the perfect time to take out the canoe, which Evan and Mya did whenever they could. Once, when they couldn't find anyone to watch their children, they decided to take the kids with them in the canoe, Izzy in her infant carrier which Mya placed at her feet, and Jeffery in his car seat that Evan placed in front of his seat in the canoe.

Afterward, Evan and Mya agreed that they probably wouldn't try to take the kids in the canoe again. As Evan walked back to his car, he couldn't help but wonder to himself, "How many memories are now in danger of not even happening?"

Chapter 5
The Memories Keep Coming

As Evan walked through the door, Jeff announced "Daddy's home!" He and Isabel ran to their father, who proceeded to give them both big hugs.

"What are you two up to?" Evan asked them.

"Playing with blocks," Jeff answered.

"Yeah," Izzy added. "I made a big pile, but Jeffery made it fall down."

"Jeffery Stewart!" Evan scolded. "Why did you do that?"

"I donno," replied Jeff, with a guilty look.

"Well, it's not very nice."

Evan continued into the kitchen where Mya was just finishing preparations for supper. "Ah, that smells good," Evan proclaimed as he grabbed the dishes to set the table. "What is it?"

"Greek Lemon Chicken," replied Mya. "My Aunt Anna's recipe."

"Sounds great," Evan replied as he laid out the utensils.

After a pause, Mya said, "So, Amy was at the cottage?"

"Yes," replied Evan. "I'll fill you in after supper. Right now, I want to get the kids seated."

He called Jeff and Izzy to the kitchen and picked Izzy up to place her in her booster seat. Jeffery sat at his usual spot across the table. When Mya placed the main dish on the table, Evan grabbed a knife and fork and took a small piece of chicken, placing it on Izzy's dish, cutting it into tiny pieces for his daughter. As Mya was serving Jeff, Evan asked his son, "So, what did you do in kindergarten today?"

"We did blocks today," Jeff replied. "Mrs. Glenn showed us how to spell our names with blocks"

"That sounds great," said Evan.

"Yeah," Jeffery continued. "I wanted to show Izzy how to spell her name in blocks."

"Is that why you asked me how to spell Izzy's name?" Mya asked.

"Yeah," replied Jeff, "but it didn't work because we only have one 'Z.'"

"Well," said Evan, "after supper I'll show you how to spell 'Isabel,' okay?"

"Okay," replied Jeff.

The usual small talk continued during the meal, but then Mya suddenly said, "Look, I know you wanted to discuss this after dinner, but please tell me, why is Amy at the cottage? She hasn't been here in such a long time."

"You're right," Evan replied. "She wants to sell the cottage."

Mya studied her husband carefully. For a moment, it looked as if he was fighting back tears. "That would be unfortunate," Mya said in a quiet voice. "What did you say to her?"

"I don't even remember," Evan replied. "I was kind of in shock."

"It's been a wonderful place to spend the summers."

"Indeed," said Evan. "Especially when your family came to visit."

Mya giggled at his comment.

For the last few years, several of Mya's relatives, parents, her sisters and brothers-in law, cousins, as well as some aunts and uncles would make the trip to Maine and Evergreen Lake on a designated weekend during the summer. Some lived in the Boston area, but most of the family made the drive from Rhode Island. As many as 25 relatives would gather at Buker Cottage, most of them sleeping in sleeping bags on the floor. Evan referred to them as "the De la Rosa clan."

Everyone would bring different types of food and drink to what would be a two-day family get-together at Buker Cottage. Mya organized the event coordinating what everyone would bring. All Evan had to worry about was making sure there was enough charcoal for the outdoor fireplace grill, and a full tank of propane for the gas grill. Both grills would be lit almost constantly throughout the two-day event. During that time, the boats would be in almost constant use, and there would always be a group of people gathered on the small beach area for swimming. But it wasn't the gathering at the lake venue that mattered so much as the gathering of the family.

"I like being at the lake," Jeffery proclaimed, and Mya could see that Evan barely managed to hold it together and avoid breaking down.

"Isn't there anything we can do?" Mya asked.

"I don't know. Tomorrow's Saturday, so I'll give her a call in the morning and meet with her later."

"Should I plan on going with you and bringing the kids?"

"Not tomorrow," Evan replied. "Maybe Sunday, if we decide to keep talking."

After putting the children to bed, Mya walked into the living room and found Evan on the sofa. He wasn't reading a book or watching TV as he normally would be doing during this time of the evening. He was simply staring at the floor.

She sat next to him and asked, "Why does she want to sell the cottage?"

After a pause, Evan replied, "She's worried about their financial situation. It's costing them thousands of dollars a month to keep my dad in the nursing home. He's not even been there a year yet, and I guess it's blown a sizable hole in their savings."

"Can't we buy the cottage?"

"Not unless you have a few hundred thousand dollars lying around."

Mya sighed. "There must be something we can do."

Evan groaned as he frustratingly exhaled. "If there is, I'm not sure what it could be."

After a pause, Evan added, "At least not yet."

Chapter 6
The Negotiation

Evan called Amy on Saturday morning, and they agreed to meet for lunch. Evan volunteered to bring lunch and they set their meeting time for one. Mya volunteered to make lunch for them, and she packed leftovers from her Greek Lemon Chicken meal that she served for supper the night before. Before Evan left, she gave him a bag containing two Tupperware microwavable containers holding the Lemon Chicken lunch. All Evan would have to do would be to warm up the containers in the microwave. Evan arrived on time, but Amy couldn't help but feel the tension between them. When Amy married Carlton, she obviously realized that Evan was a large part of the equation. She was determined to be a supportive stepmother, and over the years had developed a warm relationship with Evan. Tension between them was unusual.

When they commenced to having lunch, and upon sampling Mya's Greek chicken, Amy exclaimed, "Oh my goodness! I never realized Mya was such a great cook!"

"She certainly is," said Evan. "I tend to think she approaches cooking as an intellectual pursuit. She comes up with really creative dishes on a regular basis."

"Didn't she cook something the last time I was here?"

"No," Evan responded. "We had only gotten married a couple of months before your mother died, and she didn't cook anything when she saw how distraught I was at your mom's passing. She felt it would be better to stay with me, rather than spend her time cooking."

Amy hesitated. "I'll admit, I was partially at fault," she said. "I flew in just before the funeral, and to be honest, I couldn't fly home fast enough. I didn't realize how much her death affected you, and I should have given you more support. I'm sorry."

Evan's thoughts drifted back to his time with Marjorie after Gordon had passed away. Every morning, Marjorie would check the cabin floor for any lost pennies. She would be absolutely thrilled upon finding one, totally convinced that Gordon was looking down on her, and she might expect something good to happen during that day.

After a few moments Amy continued, "I actually thought about that last night, and it occurred to me that your being here in the summer has meant a lot more to you than it did to me, and it caused me to feel really guilty about this whole situation."

"I realize that none of this is really your fault," replied Evan. " You have a very difficult situation to deal with where my dad is concerned I'm just upset that now it's going to affect my entire family as well."

"I understand, and I want to help," Amy replied, "at least a little bit. Anyway, after spending last night feeling guilty, I called Matt Hamel, the realtor, this morning, and arranged to have breakfast with him."

"You did?" Evan asked.

"Yes, after explaining the situation to him, I asked if it would be alright for you to stay at the cottage while it was on the market. I don't think he liked the idea, but he said that he would honor my request, provided that you and your family adhere to his conditions."

"What kind of conditions?" Evan asked.

"Number 1: He will give you at least 24 hours' notice before bringing anyone in to view the property. Number 2: Upon receiving the 24-hour notice, You and the family will leave the cottage, and spend the night in your home. Number 3: Before you head home, you must make sure that the property does not show any signs of your being here. All indications that you are staying here need to be put away securely or brought home with you. There is to be no food left in the refrigerator or anywhere else. No dishes left in the sink. All clothes, whether they are clean or dirty need to be removed to your house. Matt is quite insistent that there be no signs that anyone is living here. He says that makes the property more appealing to prospective buyers. He says that if there are any signs that people are living here that it makes prospective buyers feel more like they are intruding.”

“I see,” Evan said as he rose from his chair and proceeded to walk around the room.

His gaze fell upon the archive wall, and he was surprised to see that the wall was now entirely blank. All the family’s awards, newspaper clippings, as well as Gordon’s prize largemouth bass had been completely removed from the wall.

“What happened to the archive wall?” Evan asked.

“I took everything off the wall and packed it away,” she said. “Matt’s instructions.”

“I’m not wild about that!” replied Evan. “That wall is the kind of thing that gives this place its charm.”

“Not according to Matt,” Amy pointed out.

“I see,” Evan said. “Anything else?”

“Yes,” she replied. “One more thing, and Mya’s not going to like this, but the De la Rosa family get-together is off.”

“Off?”

“Yes, off!” Amy reiterated. “During your last visit, when the two of you came to San Fran to see your father, Mya was complaining about the family event. She complained that planning for the get-together was like grabbing a tiger by the tail. But most of all, she told me that it took about a week and a half to clean up after the event.”

“I have to admit, she was pretty much right about that”

“Well, Matt says keeping the property in limbo while you two clean up for that amount of time is unacceptable.”

“Hmmm,” Evan looked lost in thought. “Alright,” he said. “If that’s the extent of Matt’s conditions, Mya and I will do our best to honor them.”

"Good! You and Mya will need to sign an agreement saying you will abide by his conditions. I will instruct Matt to draw up the agreement on Monday morning."

"An agreement? Hmmm, I guess I can do that," replied Evan. "In the meantime, what would you say to Mya and I bringing the kids over here tomorrow? After all, you haven't met them yet, and they ARE your step-Grandchildren."

"I like the sound of that. Yes, that would be great," exclaimed Amy as Evan turned to leave. "Do you think Mya would be willing to make lunch again?"

"I can ask," Evan said as he walked over to gather the two used Tupperware containers. He then turned toward the door and Amy spoke up.

"And Evan?"

"Yes?"

"While I'm glad we were able to make this arrangement, understand that if you and Mya mess up, I will have the agreement declared void, and you will have to leave. I will not let anything jeopardize the financial future of your father and I."

"I understand," Evan said as he headed out the door. "We'll see you tomorrow."

Chapter 7
Meeting the Children

On Sunday morning, the Stuart household was a rush of activity. Mya packed the lunch for their visit to the cottage after church. Meanwhile, Evan took special care in dressing the children for church while trying to explain to Jeffery about their special guest that he and Isabel would meet at the cottage after church. "You see Jeffery, when I was a little boy like you, my mommy died."

"She died?" said Jeff in an anxious voice.

"That's right," replied Evan, "and for a long, long time, I didn't have a mommy, but one day my daddy met Amy, and they fell in love and got married."

"So, she became your mommy?"

"Well, yes, I guess she did," Evan answered. "And so, she is now grandmother to you and Izzy."

"Grandmother," Jeff repeated. "My friend Jason talked about his Gramma. Is that the same thing?"

"Well, yes, it is," Evan replied.

"Jason says his Gramma gives him a lot of presents. Will I get a present from Amy?"

"Maybe for your birthday or for Christmas, but probably not today."

"Oh," Jeffery said slowly, disappointment creeping into his voice.

At that point, Mya called everyone into the kitchen, as it was time to leave. As Evan guided the minivan out of the driveway, Izzy spoke up. "Are we gonna stay with Mrs. Turner again at church today?"

"Yes," replied Evan. "You know that mommy and I are busy with the choir."

It was an understatement. Evan was the organist at St. Thomas Catholic Church in Lakeport, while Mya was the choir director. In fact, that was how the couple met. One day, as Evan was walking through the hallways at Berklee, he noticed a flyer on a bulletin board seeking a church organist at St. Anthony's Parish, which was located not far from where he was staying with Gordon and Marjorie. Always on the lookout to make extra money when he could, Evan called the pastor, who explained that the church organist at St. Anthony's was an elderly woman who was looking to cut back on her schedule. The parish decided to hire a second organist, and as such Evan's duties would be to play for weddings and other special parish events, as well as to accompany the church choir. The pastor invited Evan to the next choir rehearsal the following week and Evan accepted. The choir rehearsal was kind of an audition, and Evan passed with flying colors. Afterward, he was introduced to Mya, the choir's lead soprano and designated soloist. Mya was studying music at nearby Wellesley College and was scheduled to be a soloist for a wedding coming up the following Saturday, which Evan was now going to play for. As they rehearsed for the wedding, it was clear to both of them that they made a great team. Evan marveled at Mya's voice. It was clear, concise, with impeccable intonation and wonderful vibrato. Not only did they make a great musical team, but their personalities meshed quite well also. Beautiful, smart, and talented, Evan thought. What more could anyone ask for? The two started dating not long after, and well, the rest is history.

As they entered the dirt road to Buker Cottage, Mya brushed Izzy's hair once again. Evan thought it was overkill but decided to say nothing. Together, as a group they walked on to the front deck, and Jeffery knocked at the door. After a pause, the door opened, and Amy stood there with a big smile on her face. Mya spoke first. "Jeffery, Isabel, this is your grandmother, Amy."

Amy knelt on one knee and hugged the children. Jeffery seemed a bit standoffish meeting this stranger, despite Evan's talk with him earlier. But when Amy stood up, Izzy grabbed her leg in a tight embrace. All the adults thought it was absolutely adorable. Amy giggled and picked Isabel up to hold the child in her arms. Mustering her best "small child" voice, she said to Izzy, "Do you know you're a very pretty little girl?"

"Yes," answered Izzy, not out of ego or anything like that, but simply to be agreeable.

It took a while to warm up the lunch that Mya prepared. But finally, everyone sat down to dine. At that point, Jeffery spoke up about something that was obviously on his mind.

"Are you gonna stay with us when we come here to the cottage?" he asked Amy.

"Ohh, sweetheart, I wish I could, but I have to go home tomorrow."

"Amy lives in California, which is very, very far away," Mya explained.

"Yes," Evan added. "She has to fly on a big jet plane to get there."

"Someday I want to fly a plane," Jeffery proclaimed.

"Well," said Amy, "maybe someday you'll get your chance."

"If you do well in school," Evan added.

After lunch, Evan took the children outside to "help" him take the winter covers off the boats. Amy watched them through the window for a bit, and then said to Mya, "I can't believe how easily they accepted me."

"Well," replied Mya, "Jeffery seemed a little hesitant at first, but Isabel seemed to have no problem."

"Oh, my goodness, she's such a special child, and with Evan's eyes and your complexion, she's so adorable."

"Yes, she is," Mya agreed.

After a pause, Amy said, "I hope sometime soon you'll be able to take them to visit me in San Fran. There's so much in the Bay area I would love to take them to see."

Mya said nothing, and in a quiet voice, Amy continued. "I can also see, now that I've met them that I need to find more time to come here and visit."

"Not having the cottage might make that more difficult," Mya replied.

"I know," said Amy, "and by the way, I'm sorry to pour cold water over your family gathering, but as I'm sure Evan told you, that directive came from the real estate agent."

"Yes, I'm sure it's just a case of the agent trying to do his job."

"Yes, but I'm sure it still hurts."

"Are you sure you have to sell this place?" Mya asked with pleading eyes.

"In all honesty, I'm not sure. I only know that my first priority is to provide my husband with whatever he needs. Whatever that takes. I won't know for certain until his financial situation is resolved, but I need to be prepared for anything."

"I understand," replied Mya. "Of course, I'm sure you're aware that my first priority is my immediate family. Allowing us to stay here, even if it's only for a short time, is very gracious of you. For my family, it's almost invaluable."

Amy looked out the window one more time. The winter cover over the bicycle boat had been removed. Jeffery was sitting on the bicycle seat pretending he was navigating it on the water, his feet barely reaching the pedals. Wistfully, Amy said, "I'm beginning to see that."

Chapter 8
All Hell Breaks Loose

As Evan entered his classroom on Monday morning, he was feeling fairly optimistic. He was planning to stop by the real estate office that afternoon with Mya and the kids to sign the agreement that the realtor drew up. In a couple of weeks, school would end, and he would move the family to Buker Cottage. At that point, summer vacation would begin. He turned on his computer and pulled up his emails. His good mood vanished as the first email caught his eye. It read **FROM:** Michael Cook, Principal **TO:** LES Staff **RE:** Emergency Message. Cautiously, Evan opened the email.

To All Staff- I will be out of the school building all day today to attend an emergency meeting of all the district administrators at the Superintendent's office. We will be awaiting word from Augusta on the final budget figures reflected in the newly discovered state revenue shortfall. As some of you may have heard, the Governor has gone on record as saying that a large part of this $87 million dollar deficit is going to be met through cuts to state aid for schools, and as many of you know, the Lakeport School District is a high receiver of state aid. The superintendent believes this could mean significant cuts to our school budget for next year. I am calling an Emergency Faculty Meeting, to be held this afternoon in the school library immediately after school so I can update you on the situation. Please be prompt, and do not repeat any rumors you may hear during the school day. -M Cook

"Oh hell," Evan muttered, "white caps."

He sat back in his chair. This sounded ominous. In addition, this was not the normally friendly, jovial, supportive principal Mike Cook that everyone knew, that everyone could count on for help whenever they needed it.

Mike's email weighed on Evan all through the school day. The situation didn't seem good at all, and in the back of Evan's mind was the distinct possibility that should there be layoffs, he could end up losing his job. When his last class of the day was finishing, he was feeling antsy, and kept looking at the clock every couple of minutes. Toward the end of class someone raised their hand.

"Yes Kristen," he said. "Mr. Stuart could you tell us how you became a music teacher?"

Evan checked the clock. There were still a few minutes left in class.

"Well," he replied, "I was just about your age, when one day, during lunch time at my school, as we were waiting to return to class, I was hanging out with some of my friends that had gathered around the school piano. A couple of the kids had been taking piano lessons and they were playing songs and showing other skills that they had learned. It was right then that I decided that this was something that I wanted to learn as well, and I asked my father if I could start taking piano lessons. You see, I wasn't involved in a lot of activities like a lot of kids are today. My father enrolled me with a piano teacher and purchased a piano to practice on."

"Did your mother want you to take lessons?" asked Becky.

Evan hesitated. He didn't care for going into this part of the story, but he felt he had to be truthful. "I didn't have a mother at that time," he replied, "She died when I was eight."

"So she never heard you play?" asked Harold.

"No," said Evan, "but there were a lot of times when I would think of her when I practiced. At first, my progress was slow, but I kept at it. Each day when I returned home from school, I would do my homework, and spend the rest of my time at the piano, until my father arrived home. Practicing was the key, and eventually I became really good. When I graduated from high school, I decided to go to the Berklee College of Music in Boston. That's where I learned to be a music teacher."

"Can I learn to become a music teacher?" asked Kristen.

"I won't lie to you," replied Evan, "It takes a lot of practice, but if you're willing to do what's required, you probably can."

Evan and Brad took their usual seats toward the back of the library, while the rest of the teachers filed in and took their seats. The room was eerily quiet as Mike entered and took his place in front. There was total silence as Mike opened his folder. "The word we received from the State Education Department today is that the cut to school aid for the Lakeport district will be in the area of $325,000."

Gasps rang out across the room. These cuts were going to hurt.

"The final list of cuts will be released by the school board at their meeting tomorrow night," Mike continued. "But I have a preliminary list of cuts that the administrators approved this afternoon that I will need to share with you."

"Mike, are these cuts official?" one of the teachers asked.

"They won't be official until the school board approves them tomorrow night, but unofficially, I'm letting you know that the following cuts will most likely be approved: First, all new textbook purchases have been cut throughout the district, for a total of $42,000. Second: All supply budgets have been cut for a total of $24,000. Sorry everyone, but if you need supplies, you will probably need to provide those on your own. Third: all equipment and furniture purchases have been cut for a total of $30,000."

"There go my new desks," mused the second-grade teacher.

Mike continued, "Forth: In transportation, there will be a re-shuffling of bus routes, which should result in a reduction in transportation costs, also, all field trips have been eliminated. Sorry Brad."

Brad raised his hand. "Hey Mike, if I can make enough money through fund raising to afford my field trip, would that be allowable?"

"I'm afraid it would be problematic," Mike replied. "The school board has anticipated that many teachers may try to do fundraising to make up for these cuts. They are fearful that the community may become overwhelmed by fundraisers. Therefore, it is expected that the school board will pass a new policy at their meeting tomorrow night that all fundraisers need to be approved by the board. Only a fraction of the fundraiser requests are expected to receive approval."

Brad groaned in frustration.

"Finally," Mike continued, "there are three retirements in the district, two at the high school and one in the middle school. Those positions will go unfilled resulting in a savings of $131,000. However, that's still not enough to close the budget gap. In order to do that, the superintendent believes it will be necessary to lay off four staff members."

"Are any of us going to be laid off?" someone asked.

"That will be announced at the school board meeting tomorrow night. Right now, I don't know any more than you do."

Steve, the teachers' union representative, who had been quiet up to this point, spoke up. "Mike, do we know if any maintenance cuts are on the table?"

"As far as I know it's on the table," Mike replied, "but I don't know where it stands. Any other questions?"

No one spoke up.

"Alright," Mike continued, "I'm going to suggest that as many of you as possible attend tomorrow night's meeting. The meeting will be held in the high school cafeteria starting at 7pm. If I'm put in a position where I have to defend our teachers or our programs, I may need help from some of you. Okay, that will do it. Thank you very much everyone."

With that, Mike left the room, and most of the other teachers got up to leave as well. Brad turned to Mike and said, "What do you think?"

"I'm worried," Evan replied. "There's the old adage 'When it comes to lay-offs, the music teachers are usually the first to go.'"

"Well, let's hope that's not true."

"It happens enough so that a lot of people believe it."

In fact, it was an adage that bothered Evan a lot. Evan believed that what kids learned in his classroom was just as important as what they learned in other classes. It was a shame that many lay people did not share that belief.

"Oh, by the way, while I think of it, can you find some time within the next few days to stop over at the cottage and help me put the dock in the water?"

"Yeah, no problem," Brad said, "I'll give you a call."

Chapter 9
"The Plan"

Mya recruited a neighbor to watch the kids while she and Evan went to see Matt Hamel, Amy's realtor. Evan was silent on the way to the real estate office, not wanting to talk about the prospect of layoffs for fear of upsetting Mya. As soon as they entered the office, Matt came forward and introduced himself, shaking hands with both of them and guiding them to the conference room. As they sat down, Matt produced the agreement that he had drafted, and said to them, "This is just a formality, but as a notary, I need to see both of your ID's."

Evan and Mya took out their driver's licenses and passed them to Matt. Matt examined them and nodded, handing them back. "Again, I apologize, I'm afraid it's required."

"Not a problem," Evan said.

"To be honest," Matt continued, "I was opposed to this idea when Amy brought it up, but she made such a passionate case for you that I realized we needed to find a way to make it happen."

"Well, we're glad you did," Mya replied.

Matt went through all the details of the agreement with them, and then presented the paper to Evan and Mya for them to sign. As he was signing the document, Evan said, "Matt, you've been a realtor here for a significant number of years, correct?"

"A year from this November it'll be 20 years, but don't say it too loud, it makes me feel old."

Mya laughed, but Evan remained serious.

"I'm inclined to believe that during that time, you might have seen some creative ways in which folks have been able to finance and purchase properties, no?"

"Well, yes, I've seen a few unique instances over the years. I'm guessing you would be open to creative ideas to purchase the cottage?"

"We would," Evan replied.

"Well, actually, Amy was way ahead of you, and told me she would much rather sell the cottage to you as opposed to someone else. After talking with her, I gave the idea some thought, and yeah, I think I may have come up with a hairbrained plan in which several dominoes would need to fall properly, but it just could work."

"Really?" Mya asked. Her voice sounding more hopeful than it had in a long time.

"Now, don't get your hopes up," Matt cautioned. "A lot of things would have to go right, and it would require some sacrifices on your part. Let me ask you first, how much equity do you have in your current residence?"

"Well," said Evan, "we bought the house seven years ago with a down payment of 25 thousand, so I'm guessing somewhere between 25 and 30 thousand."

"That's probably correct," Matt responded, "and it just might be enough."

"To do what?" Evan asked. "This is where the hairbrained part comes in. If I can sell YOUR house, that would free up your equity, and if Amy would agree to it, use the equity to winterize the cottage so that your family could live there year around."

"That would be incredible!" Evan exclaimed.

"But wait," Mya interjected, "how exactly would that work? I'm sensing that this is where the sacrifice part comes in."

"Besides," Evan added, "wouldn't that interfere with your selling the cottage?"

"That wouldn't matter, because if this plan were to work as I envision, Amy would be selling the place to you."

"I don't understand how that would work," Mya said with a puzzled voice.

Matt continued, "Look, I had a long talk with Amy about her husband, well, your dad."

Matt nodded to Evan. "Once they all figure out how to resolve the financial issues, I don't think the situation is going to be quite as dire as Amy fears it will be."

"That would be good," said Evan.

"Yes, it would," replied Matt. "That leads to the next step of this hairbrained idea. Amy would have to be convinced to sell you the property through a lease-purchase agreement."

"A what?" Mya asked.

"A lease-purchase agreement. Essentially, instead of the monthly mortgage payment that you now make every month, you would be making a similar payment to Amy every month as rent. However, each monthly rental payment would be deducted from the purchase price, and eventually you will have paid the full selling price."

"I've never heard of this type of agreement," said Mya.

"It's a lot more common than people think," Matt explained. "I know of a couple of realtors that make their living exclusively through lease-purchase agreements. In some circles, it's also known as 'Rent-to-Own.'"

"Interesting," said Evan.

"I'll tell you what," Matt continued. "Why don't the two of you give this whacko idea some thought. If you think you want to give it a try, give me a call, and we can set up a time so I can come over and view your property. We can come up with a realistic estimate of a possible selling price."

"That sounds like a plan," Evan said, shaking Matt's hand.

Mya added, "Thank you very much," as they turned to leave.

As they headed home, Mya said, "What do you think?"

"It's a complicated plan. I sure as hell want to give it a lot of thought before we slap a FOR SALE sign on the house."

"Agreed," stated Mya as they turned on to their street. Evan did not share with Mya his real thoughts, that selling the house without a job would make things a lot more complicated.

Chapter 10
The Board Meeting

As Evan entered Lakeport High School, there was a note on the door saying that the school board meeting had been moved to the auditorium. Apparently, the board was anticipating a large crowd, and Evan was certain they were correct. As he entered the auditorium, he picked up a copy of the agenda. The agenda was not very long. The first item was a resolution for a new fundraising policy. That was followed by resolutions for proposed budget cuts followed by opening the floor for public comments, and finally, votes on all the resolutions. Evan saw that they had only allowed 30 minutes for public comments. That wasn't going to fly. Evan sensed that despite the short agenda, this was going to be a long evening. He looked around the auditorium. It was about half full, with more people streaming in by the minute. Most of the elementary school staff had gathered on the left side, about half-way down. Evan decided not to join them. If his worst fears were about to happen, he didn't want anyone around him, should it occur.

Exactly at 7pm, the school board members entered the stage as well as the superintendent. They took their seats, then Jody Hall, chairwoman of the board walked to the podium and called the meeting to order. After the Pledge of Allegiance, she patiently waited while everyone sat down, and the volume of the room had toned down.

Then she started to speak. "Good evening, everyone, and welcome to tonight's school board meeting. I have to say that in my 10 years serving on this board, we have never had to deal with as unpleasant a task as we are faced with this evening. We were as shocked by this budget development as you were, and I speak for the entire board when I say that we truly regret what we are required to do tonight. We are your friends and neighbors, but we have a job to do this evening, which is to balance our school budget so that we don't cause any overt tax increases to our citizens."

"Allow me to recap. Last week, independent auditors examining the state sales tax records discovered that sales tax revenues had fallen sharply going back to last summer. Actual sales tax collections fell significantly short of projections, and the end result is that an 87-million-dollar budget deficit had developed. The state legislature and the governor were forced to adopt a new state budget cutting eighty-seven million dollars from the already approved state budget. Among other things, the state included major cuts to state school aid. Yesterday, we were informed that the state school aid to the Lakeport School District was cut by $325,000. Now, as many of you know, we met back in March to approve a school budget for the Lakeport Schools for the next school year. However, that budget was based on the old state school aid figures, and tonight, it will be our unpleasant duty to cut $325,000 from next year's school budget. Various resolutions will be proposed tonight in order to accomplish this task. We will then hear comments from the public, followed by a vote on the resolutions. However, before we get to that, we have a resolution proposal regarding fundraising policy. The chair recognizes superintendent Eric Smith."

The superintendent rose, and outlined the new fundraising proposal under which all fundraising proposals would have to be submitted to the school board. It was exactly as Mike had outlined in the faculty meeting the day before. After the fundraising resolution, the budget resolutions followed. Each time, the chair would recognize the superintendent, who would make a resolution cutting a budget category. Again, it unfolded exactly as Mike had predicted in the faculty meeting: Textbooks, Supplies, Equipment and Furniture, Transportation. Then, in a move Evan did not anticipate, the superintendent outlined a resolution proposing a $53,000 cut in Maintenance. Then came the proposal to leave the three retirement positions unfilled. Finally, one resolution remained, the one that Evan was dreading.

The superintendent said, "If it please the board, it is recommended that in order to close the budget gap that three staff positions be eliminated through layoffs, a Special Ed. teachers aid at the middle school, the elementary librarian position and the elementary music position."

Evan wasn't surprised, but he was still devastated. He sat back in his chair and exhaled loudly. The chairwoman then opened the public comment portion of the meeting, and the first person to the microphone was Mike Cook.

"Ladies and gentlemen of the board," he said, "I know you have to make cuts somewhere, but I would urge you to reevaluate your decision regarding the elementary layoffs. I think I can say with some degree of authority that such budget cuts are more keenly felt at the elementary level as opposed to the upper grades. I believe our students will suffer to a greater degree than middle school or high school students. Mrs. Dansk is an invaluable resource for both students and staff, and you only need to listen to our choir and band in the elementary school to realize that Mr. Steward has done an exemplary job with our students. I implore you to reexamine your decision regarding these positions. Thank you."

Other speakers followed. Others, including some parents took the same position as Mike questioning the elementary layoffs. Then, Evan held his breath as Marcellus Gagnon approached the microphone. Marcellus was a self-appointed "star" of public meetings in Lakeport. If there was a public meeting that included public comments, he would be there to speak. He took what Evan felt was an extremely conservative view of fiscal issues, believing that a municipality such as Lakeport should spend as little as possible in order to hold down taxes. He considered several subject areas taught in the schools to be unnecessary, including music.

"Ladies and gentlemen of the board," he began, "I'm here to speak in support of the proposed layoffs and make some additional suggestions as well. To begin with, I don't understand why a special education teacher, who generally works with individual students and small groups needs an assistant. To me, that makes no sense at all. I also don't believe we need an elementary librarian. Surely, classroom teachers can assist students picking out books to read as well as a librarian can. Also, not only do I support cutting the elementary music position, but I would like to see you cut the elementary art and physical education teachers as well to save the school district additional money. Those positions are not necessary at the elementary level, and it's through over-spending such as this that has put us in the dismal financial position that we face tonight. As a voter and taxpayer, I urge you to act on my suggestions. Thank You."

Evan knew that if he were standing next to Marcellus right now, he would punch him in the nose. He thought back to a saying that one of his professors used a lot, "You can't fix stupid."

Fortunately, no one on the board reacted. Through experience, they understood that the best way to handle Marcellus was to simply move on after he spoke. But it still felt to Evan that the negative comments had an impact.

"Just what I need," he muttered under his breath, "more whitecaps."

The following two speakers came to the mic to rebut the comments made by Marcellus. Other speakers that followed lamented the position eliminations in the high school and middle school. When Steve, the elementary union rep. came to the microphone, he questioned the board on something else.

"Ladies and gentlemen of the board," he said. "I would like to question you on a budget item that appears to have been overlooked. As I understand it, we are scheduled to spend $400,000. on a new roof for the middle school this summer. Is it possible that we might find a cheaper alternative to fixing those leaks? Even a savings of, say, $100,000. might be enough to avoid lay-offs completely."

"The board did examine that option," replied Jody Hall, the chairwoman. "We were told that it's not possible, that the roof is in such poor shape that a cheaper alternative will not work."

The chair kept the public comment portion open for another 30 minutes, but at that point the arguments had become rather cyclical, and the chairwoman put an end to the debate. The voting commenced on all of the resolutions. One by one, each resolution was approved by voice vote, including the final resolution which included the layoffs. Evan sat with his head in his hand as the chairwoman thanked everyone and adjourned the meeting. As people got up to leave, Evan saw Mike and Steve rise together and start walking over toward him. Mike leaned down so that he was close to Evan's ear and said, "Can you be in my office at 7:15 tomorrow morning?"

Evan nodded, afraid to speak, for fear he might break down in tears. Steve leaned down toward Evan's other ear and said, "We're going to help you all we can."

Evan very dryly said, "Thank you," and the two headed for the door.

Evan left shortly after. Although he told Mya about the meeting before he left, now he was going to have to give her the bad news. It was going to be a long night.

Chapter 11
An Unexpected Development

Evan walked into Mike's office at precisely 7:15. Mike was already there waiting for him, as well as Steve. Evan was tired, and it showed. He and Mya talked until well past midnight, and even then, the two of them lay in bed, wide awake for most of the night.

Evan sat down, and Mike said, "You're going to receive a lay-off notice in your box sometime this afternoon, but that doesn't mean that you're toast just yet."

"Why not?" Evan asked.

"There's been a development," said Steve. "We couldn't talk about it last night because it was kind of sensitive."

"Barbara Walker, the middle school music teacher is also going to receive a lay-off notice today," said Mike.

"I don't understand," Evan said with puzzlement creeping into his voice. "I thought the reason I was targeted was because I have the least seniority of any of the music staff."

"That's what we all thought," replied Mike, "but yesterday afternoon, I received a call from the superintendent. It seems that he was going through the personnel records to confirm the music staff seniorities, when something jumped out at him."

"You may remember," continued Steve, "that five years ago, Barbara applied for a sabbatical to finish her master's degree."

"Yes," replied Evan, "I remember it vaguely."

"Well," continued Mike, "the school board turned down her request because she didn't qualify for a sabbatical."

"She only started in Lakeport a year before you did," added Steve.

"When the board turned down her sabbatical, she amended her request to take a year off as unpaid leave," Mike explained. "The board granted that request, but unpaid leave does not count toward seniority. That means that the both of you are tied for seniority in the Lakeport School District."

"Hmmm," murmured Evan, finally understanding where this was going.

"There is a section in the union contract that deals with exactly this type of situation," explained Steve, "although this is the first time it is being invoked."

"The contract reads that the board will choose a date for back-to-back hearings involving the two of you," Mike continued. "You will each state your case as to why you shouldn't be the person laid-off."

"We will assist you in making your case as much as we can," Steve said.

"Right!" Mike jumped in. "We don't want you going anywhere. We want you right here where you belong."

"Thank you very much," Evan replied.

"Alright," Mike said looking at the clock. "Unless you have any questions, why don't you head back to your room, and try to catch a 10-minute cat nap before your classes start."

Evan smiled and thanked the both of them. He headed back to his room with a new spring in his step. As he walked into his room, he pulled out his cell phone and called Mya. "Hi Honey," he said, "there's been a development."

Evan arrived home to find the children playing in the yard. The weather was now warm enough to play in their sandbox, and they both seemed content playing there. As Evan approached the sandbox, the children shouted together, "Daddy's home!" and ran over to their father.

Evan gave them the standard hugs that he always gave. However, based on the amount of dirt on their clothes, not to mention their hands and faces, it was clear that they had been in the sandbox for some time. It would take an extensive clean-up as well as a change of clothes to get them ready for supper.

"Where's Mommy?" he asked.

"She went inside!" replied Izzy.

"Yeah," added Jeff. "Her cell phone went off, I think it was VoVo."

The name that the children called Mya's mother. "She started crying," Izzy said matter of factly.

Leave it to young children with no filter to not even realize when they're tattling.

"Alright," Evan said, "here's what we're going to do. You can stay in the sand box for a few more minutes while I go see mommy. Then, I'm going to call you both inside so we can clean up for supper."

"Aww!" Jeffery moaned, "Can't I show you the roads that I made for my truck?"

"Maybe later," Evan answered as he turned toward the door.

As Evan entered the hallway there was silence. Then he heard Mya's voice. She sounded somewhat exasperated. "Yes Mom, you're right, I think it's wonderful that Aunt Julia has found a way to prepare Peri Peri Chicken for the grill, but as I've been telling you, this wasn't our decision, it was forced on us. We just can't do it."

At that point, she noticed Evan walking into the kitchen, and spoke into the phone, "Look Ma, I have to go. Evan's home and we have to get the kids ready for supper. . . Yes, I will call you later. . . Yes, I'll tell him. . . Yes, bye-bye."

She hung up and faced Evan. As Evan hugged her, she started sobbing.

"I think the family's been burning up the phone lines all afternoon. I feel so bad!"

"It's not your fault," Evan said as he hugged her tightly.

When the embrace finished, she said, "Evan, I don't know about these restrictions. It's going to feel like we have one foot in the cottage and the other foot in this house."

"I know," Evan replied as he still held her by the shoulders. "Maybe. . . Maybe we should consider not making the move to the cottage."

Mya frowned. This certainly was a suggestion she would never have expected Evan to make. "Absolutely not!" she said. "It wouldn't be fair to the children, nor would it be fair to us."

"Are you certain we can make this work?" asked Evan cautiously.

"I'm sure we can," replied Mya, "but it's going to be hard, especially if the cottage sells.

Chapter 12
Whitecaps

The following evening, Evan drove the minivan containing the family as they headed for Buker Cottage. As the minivan approached the dirt road to Buker Cottage, Evan's heart sank. There posted on the side of the road was a FOR SALE sign from Matt Hamel's office. "Oh Hell," Evan mumbled as he made the turn. Another FOR SALE sign greeted them as they approached the cottage.

After parking the vehicle, Mya took the kids inside the cottage, while Evan, toolbox in hand, made his way down toward the water. He looked out at the lake as he approached the shoreline. There was a brisk breeze blowing across the water, and in the distance, Evan could see dark clouds gathering. In the middle of the lake, the waves had kicked up, and Evan could see several whitecaps.

"Looks like a storm," Evan said to himself. "How appropriate."

There wasn't much involved in terms of preparing the dock. Evan only needed to check the bracing and leg posts for loose connections. Evan had thought that someday, when the kids were older, he might add additional sections on to the dock. But now, that idea was in limbo. In its current form, the dock itself was fairly simple. A pre-made deck sixteen feet long and four feet wide. One end would be attached to a small concrete slab on the land, that Evan installed himself. The other end had longer leg posts for the deeper water, with a set of 24" wheels attached. The wheels were designed to take on water as they were wheeled into the lake. This would provide the dock with more stability. The quiet was broken by someone calling his name. Evan turned his head to see Brad walking down the path toward the shore.

"Behold, I bring gifts!" Brad proclaimed as he approached, holding up a small plastic bag.

"Really?" responded Evan, making the final adjustment to the dock leg.

"Indeed, Melanie was at the dollar store the other day when she saw these solar lights," Brad said as he pulled the lights out of the bag. "She says that when she saw them in the store, she immediately thought of you and how we crashed into the dock on that really dark night last year."

"It wasn't a crash!" Evan argued. "It was just a tap."

"Uh-hunn," Brad responded. "Well, perhaps we can tape these to the end posts, so that you can avoid any more . . 'taps.'"

Evan laughed and said, "Yeah, right! Well, please thank Melanie for me."

"Will do. Well, it looks like I arrived just in time. Is this puppy ready to go?"

"Indeed, it is," Evan responded. "Why don't you take the left side, and I'll take the right."

Rolling the dock into the water was a fairly simple task. All that remained was to connect the dock to the concrete slab.

"Looks like another mission accomplished Margo-sub," Brad said.

Evan thought about it for a moment. Now was as good a time as any for a little intervention. "You know," he said, "At some point you're going to need to put that name on the shelf."

"You're probably right," Brad replied, "but sometimes it seems as if it's the only thread I have to remember her by. I'm sure you realize that if it hadn't been for fate, I may well have married her."

"Look," argued Evan, "When she was killed, it was devastating for both of us, and I realize it affected you more than me. But it's been almost five years. Surely you married Melanie because you fell in love with her."

"Yes, yes I did," replied Brad. "But every now and then, we come across a situation where I end up making comparisons between her and Melanie." Exasperation was creeping into his voice. "I know it's not fair, but I can't help it."

After a pause, Evan said in a quiet voice, "You have to try. If you can't get over it, her memory is going to haunt your marriage indefinitely. You're going to be a father soon, and right now, the only problem of the day ought to be the fact that Mya hasn't decided what to give Melanie for her shower."

After a pause, he continued, "Maybe you need some help with this. Why don't you talk with Lisa."

"The guidance counselor?"

"Yeah, she's trained in grief counseling. I don't think it would hurt."

"Hmmm, I'll think about it."

After a moment, Brad chuckled and said, "It's ironic, here you are in danger of losing your job, and you're the one trying to help me instead of the reverse."

"Well," Evan replied, "in my case it's kind of like whitecaps on the lake, a sign of bad weather ahead."

Brad laughed, "You would use a lake analogy, no wonder you love this place."

At that point, Brad's phone went off. He checked it and said, "Oh hell! We have a call!"

Brad was a member of the volunteer fire department, and someone had reported a fire.

"Go ahead," said Evan, "and thanks for your help."

"No problem!" Brad replied as he headed up the path.

"And be careful, DADDY," Evan shouted.

Brad smiled as he turned back and hurried up to his car.

When Evan finished connecting the dock, he grabbed his toolbox, and headed into the cottage. Mya had saved a tuna sandwich for him, and there was just enough Kool-Aid for one more glass. The kids, having long lost interest in their toys, were sitting at the table with their mother working on a jigsaw puzzle.

"How did it go?" Mya asked as he sat down.

"Just fine," Evan responded. "But I have this feeling of dread that I may have put the dock in the water for the very last time."

Chapter13
Amy's News

It was almost mid-afternoon when Mya's cell phone rang. Isabel was napping, and Jeffery would soon arrive home on the bus. Mya activated the phone and said "Hello?"

"Hello Mya, it's Matt Hamel" said the voice at the other end. "I just wanted to let you know that I'll be bringing some people over to view the cottage on Saturday. We should arrive there at about 11am. I hope that's not a problem."

"No, it's not." Actually, Mya was not being truthful. The previous day, Evan had stopped by the marina to purchase some Marine Paint. His plan was to paint the motorboat on Saturday to prepare it for the water. He also had planned to repair a deck railing that had become loose during the winter. Now, they would have to change their plans.

"Thanks for letting us know," she said.

"No problem," replied Matt. "Tell me, have you two discussed my crazy plan at all?"

"We're still talking about it." Again, she was not being truthful. With Evan's job in limbo, Matt's plan just didn't seem reasonable.

"Well," Matt said, "if you have any questions, don't hesitate to give me a call."

"We won't Matt. Thank you very much." With that, Mya turned off the phone, and said out loud, "And so, it has begun."

With a loud sigh, she placed the phone on the table and went to the front door to watch for Jeffery's bus.

Izzy woke up from her nap just as Jeff was coming in the front door.

"How was school today?" Mya asked as Jeffery hung up his backpack.

"It was okay. Can we take out our crayons?" he asked. "I wanna draw an airplane."

"I wanna draw too!" added Izzy.

"Alright," Mya responded. "I'll get you some paper."

Once the children were settled at the kitchen table, Mya turned her attention to starting dinner, but before she was able to do anything, the cell phone rang again. She walked into the living room before activating the phone.

"Hi Amy," she said.

"Hello Mya, I knew I couldn't bother Evan at school, but I had to call to tell you, they've made a breakthrough with Carlton."

"A breakthrough?"

"That's right!" replied Amy. "They say he showed the first indications while I was out visiting you, but now it's progressed to where he can move his left foot and bend his left leg slightly."

"That sounds wonderful Amy."

"It is, it is," she replied, "but there's more. He can write! He can move his left hand and hold a pencil. He can write!"

"Write? you mean on paper?"

"Yes, the therapists, those stinkers, they kept it under wraps from me, but when I arrived at his room yesterday, they were waiting for me, which was strange, because they usually do their sessions with him in the morning, before visiting hours. Yesterday, they had placed a pad of paper under Carlton's left hand before I arrived. When I entered his room, Carlton started tapping on the pad of paper, which was amazing in itself, but then Gil, one of the therapists, placed a pencil in his hand and he started writing."

"With his left hand? Is he left-handed?" Mya asked.

"No," said Amy, "and to be honest, his writing is hard to read, kind of like hen scratches. And each time he writes a single letter, Gil has to lift his arm and move the pad so he can write the next letter."

"That's still quite amazing," Mya said.

Amy could hardly contain her excitement. "Absolutely! Do you know what he wrote? It was so sweet! He wrote 'HI I LUV U.'"

"That's amazing!"

"Yes, I'm so happy, I can't get over it."

"You shouldn't have to," Mya replied, "it's nothing short of miraculous."

"Now listen, you simply have to bring the children out here to visit him as soon as school vacation starts!"

"UUUMMH, Amy? I'm afraid that's going to be a problem."

When Mya finished explaining Evan's job situation, there was a long pause on the other end. Finally, Amy spoke, "I understand. Listen, Mya, don't worry about getting out here. You and Evan go ahead and deal with this matter. If Evan gets laid-off, I'm certain he can find another position."

"I certainly hope so," replied Mya.

"You should think about sending out applications yourself," said Amy. "Aren't you certified in Maine?"

"No, but I wouldn't have any problem if I applied. Still, I'm not wild about the idea of Evan being a Stay-at-Home dad."

"You need to have all options on the table and see what will work best. I don't know if I'll be able to help you or not, but if I can, I will."

"We may hold you to that," Mya said. After Mya hung up the phone, she looked at the clock. "No fancy recipes tonight!" she mused to herself. "Looks like hamburgers are on this evening's menu."

The superintendent's conference room door closed behind Evan, and he exhaled loudly. He realized that Mike and Steve had done a good job preparing him for his school board hearing. They had anticipated many of the questions from the school board members quite accurately, and Evan was ready with prepared answers. The only question he hadn't anticipated came from the Superintendent, Eric Smith, who said, "Mr. Stuart, I noticed that you were present at the school board meeting the other night. I'm sure you heard Mr.

Marcellus Gagnon's comments regarding music in the elementary curriculum. I curious to know what your thoughts are on those comments."

Evan thought for a moment but had no problem constructing his response. "All respect to Mr. Gagnon," he began, "but he clearly does not understand the role that music plays in the education of young students. Music has been identified as one of Gardiner's seven intelligences. Students in their first few years of school are best equipped to understand musical concepts, and it is well established through a very large amount of research that those musical concepts assist students in learning concepts in other subject areas. Moreover, the elementary music curriculum is the cornerstone of building a successful music program throughout the K-12 system. To serve the students the best we can, a sound program infrastructure in music needs to be maintained in all the grades."

The board gave no indication how it would rule, but Evan was very satisfied with the answer he gave.

Chapter 14
The Last School Day

The bulletin boards were bare. Maps were rolled up and stored. All artwork and pictures had been removed from the walls. Electronic equipment was locked away in storage rooms. The last day of the school year was bittersweet. For the students, the end of a chapter, as well as the exuberance of moving on to the next grade. For teachers, a well-deserved rest, but knowing that in a couple of months the building would come roaring back to life. But for Evan, the feelings were different. Every final task was laced in sadness. As he put away materials, he knew he would not be taking them out again, at least not in this building.

The first segment of the day involved the students cleaning out their desks and passing in their textbooks. Meanwhile, Evan was in the gym, preparing for the final school assembly. He moved the piano in place and set up the chairs and music stands for the band. He had offers of help, but he didn't take anyone up on it. He ended up doing it himself, fighting back tears in the process. As he was finishing, Mike came up to him to go over a few details involving the assembly.

At the end of the conversation, Evan said, "Look, Mike, I'm going to hide in the locker room until it's time for the assembly to start."

"The locker room?" replied Mike.

"I don't want to be dealing with any parents or anything like that, and during the assembly, I don't know if you were planning to give me any recognition, but under the circumstances, I'd prefer that you didn't."

"As you wish," assured Mike.

At that point, the school intercom chirped on, and everyone could hear Mrs. Branch announce, "Mr. Cook, you have a phone call."

"Oops, I better get to that," said Mike as he started walking away.

Evan sighed as he finished setting up the last few music stands. He had found a penny on the bedroom floor as he was dressing that morning. Evan never thoroughly bought into the belief that Gordon and Marjorie held regarding lost pennies. "I can't imagine anything good coming out of today." he mused to himself. Brad was the first teacher to bring his class down to the gym for the assembly. The band and choir students from the other grades were also arriving. Evan set up the choir students on the choral risers and checked that the band students were seated properly with their instruments and music. Satisfied that everything was in place, he said to Brad, "I'm headed for the locker room."

Brad nodded. Evan had asked Brad to watch over the band and choir while he was in the locker room since many of the music students were from his class, and Brad agreed.

It didn't take long for parents to arrive and take their places in the bleachers. The rest of the classrooms followed, teachers directing their students to sit on the floor. Evan opened the locker room door and peered out. The kindergarten class was seated at the front, while the other classes were seated behind them. Jeffery was seated in the first row of Kindergarteners, most of them looking about the gym wide-eyed while their older school mates were jovial and somewhat antsy. Evan realized that this was a new experience for the Kindergarteners and for such young kids, processing the whole scene was a challenge.

Right on time, Mike stepped in front of the podium with the microphone and welcomed everyone. After some opening remarks, he introduced the kindergarten teachers to present awards. Evan always marveled at the lengths that the teachers would go through to give awards to as many kids as possible. Evan opened the locker room door a bit more so he could look out into the audience. He spotted Mya sitting in the far corner of the bleachers near the door, with Izzy sitting on her lap. When Jeffery's name was announced for a spelling award, he saw his son march proudly up to receive his certificate, his face beaming. Evan looked at Mya, and she was smiling as well. There's no feeling like being a proud parent.

Soon, it was time for the band to play, and Evan walked on to the gym floor and took his place in front of the band. After checking that he had the attention of all of the band members, he started the piece titled "A Royal March." The students played well, and after the piece was over, he had the students stand for the applause, and then he bowed to the audience. As the applause subsided, he turned to the band and said, "Good Job!" and then walked over to the piano. About 20 minutes later, it was time for the choir to sing. He looked at the choir, seated on the choral risers and raised his hand. After making sure that he had the attention of all the choir members, he signaled them to stand up together. He played the introduction on the piano, and the choir began singing "The Graduation Song." The song was actually a melody from a Haydn symphony, but at some point in time, someone wrote lyrics to the melody based on graduation, and it was published. The students sang well, and when the song ended, Evan stood and gestured to the choir during the applause before bowing to the audience. After some final awards, the assembly came to an end. The students were excused to go home with their parents, or board the buses that had just arrived. Mya walked over to Evan and kissed him on the cheek. Isabel, although her mother was holding her, reached out to Evan to give him a hug. In no time Jeffery had found his way to them.

Evan reached his hand down for a high five and said, "Hey Buddy, Good Job!"

Jeff smacked his father's hand and was all smiles.

Mya said to the kids, "Do you two want to help daddy put away the music stands?"

"Yes," the children said in unison, and they all walked toward the band set-up. Izzy had a difficult time handling the music stands, so Mya instructed Jeff to help his sister. Together, they carried one stand at a time to the storage room.

In the middle of the process, the intercom chirped on once again. "Mr. Stuart, you have a phone call."

Evan frowned as he turned to Mya, "Who could that be?"

Evan rarely received phone calls through the main office. His friends and acquaintances usually called him on his cell. "There's only one way to find out," said Mya.

Evan started toward the office hoping that the caller wasn't some salesman.

Chapter 15
The Phone Call

As Evan approached the main office, Mike was waiting for him and said, "Take it in my office."

Evan nodded as he walked through the doorway. He went into Mike's office, sat at the desk, and picked up the phone.

"Evan Stuart," he said.

"Haayyy Evan!" exclaimed the voice at the other end. "It's Ollie!"

"Hi Ollie," Evan replied.

Oliver Iverson was the music teacher at Lakeport High School. Evan really liked him and thought he was an outstanding teacher. He had observed Ollie's classes a couple of times. Although he talked as if he was a refugee from the beatnik days, he could be a very demanding teacher. But he managed to make his classes fun, and the high school kids loved him for it. "OOOH Man, you're not going to believe it, but the superintendent has given me the honor of calling you with the good news!"

"Good news? What good news?"

"OOOH, the best news dude! Are you sitting down?"

"Yes, what news?"

"Your school board hearing has been rendered moot pal. Your layoff notice has been rescinded. As of this morning, Barbara Walker submitted her resignation."

"She resigned?"

"That's right dude! She took a position in Massachusetts."

"Really?"

"Yuuuup, she actually applied for the position before all this budget stuff happened. She wanted to be closer to her family."

"So, I can keep my job here at the elementary school?"

"Wellll, sort of. That's the not so good part of the news. With her gone, that means that her position is the music position that gets cut. But we can't leave a hole that size in the music curriculum. As a result, that leaves only the two of us to cover all of the music classes in the district."

"The two of us? I don't understand. How is that supposed to work?"

"We have to restructure the curriculum man! I just got out of a looong meeting with the superintendent. We have to eliminate classes in all three schools. The high school has already been told to eliminate my guitar class, my music history class, and my jazz choir. You will still be teaching band and choir at the elementary school, but Mike has been told to reduce your general music classes by 50%."

"50%?" said Evan. "That's a big cut."

"It's unavoidable man," Ollie replied. "I'm going to be teaching the middle school band classes. We need you to teach the middle school choir."

"I can do that."

"Good! Next year, we'll ask the school board to restore the cut music position, but until then dude, it's just you and me, the Dynamic Duo."

Evan laughed. "Ollie, you have a gift for making bad news sound good."

Now it was Ollie's turn to laugh. "Yeah man, but it also means we'll be spending hours planning this restructure."

"What say you meet me in my room on Tuesday at 9:30? I'll bring the coffee."

"And I'll bring the donuts," replied Evan. "See you then. Thanks Ollie."

"Congratulations Evan, Well, sort of. Bye."

As Evan hung up the phone, it was as if a great weight had been lifted from his shoulders.

"It's going to be a lot of work," Evan thought to himself, "but it will be worth it. Wait until I tell Mya."

As Evan walked into the gym, Mya was standing in the middle of the floor, smiling at him. Standing next to her was Mike, who was also smiling. Evan walked up to them.

"It appears someone spilled the beans," Evan said, with an amused look on his face.

"Couldn't help it," replied Mike as he reached to shake Evan's hand.

"I'm so glad you're staying with us. Come see me after lunch."

"Will do," replied Evan as Mike walked away. Evan hugged Mya, gave her a kiss, and said, "I think it's time we gave Matt Hamel a call."

Chapter 16
The Beach Day

The children were excited as Evan drove the family in the minivan toward Evergreen Lake. Jeff and Izzy were in their bathing suits. Izzy held her plastic sand pail on her lap with a small shovel. Jeff had his toy dump truck and toy bulldozer. As an alternative to going to Buker Cottage, the family had decided to spend Saturday morning at Koasek Beach, the same beach that Brad and Evan had taken Brad's 5th grade class to. Mya had the beach blanket and towels for everyone. Evan had previously loaded the beach umbrella and a couple of beach chairs. As they approached the entrance to the parking lot, Mya took note of the Beach sign. "'Koasek', that's a strange name for a beach."

"Not that much," replied Evan. "I researched it."

"Of course, you did," said his wife.

"Koasek is from the Abnaki language which is spoken by the Native American tribes in Maine. It means 'Where the small pines are.' It's probably the closest Native American reference to the English word Evergreen."

"You are such a font of information," said Mya as they pulled into a parking space.

As Mya was unbuckling the children from their car seats, Evan went to open the tailgate. As soon as the children were unbuckled, they started to take off toward the beach.

"STOP!" Mya shouted and the children froze. "No one's going anywhere until we put on sunscreen."

Reluctantly, Jeff and Izzy turned back toward the minivan. As Evan was unloading the umbrella and beach chairs, he took in his surroundings. The sun was shining as it would any mid-June day, although there were several clusters of white and gray clouds scattered across the sky, and what looked like a thunderhead in the distance. The beach was maybe at one quarter capacity, although it was still mid-morning. More people would arrive as the day went on. He looked over to the boat ramp that was next to the beach. About a half-dozen empty boat trailers sat in the trailer parking area, while two more boats sat on their trailers near the ramp as their owners made preparations to launch them. The family walked together until they reached the sand. At that point, the children lost all restraint, and started running toward the water. They both knelt at the water's edge and started digging in the sand. Evan and Mya chose a spot where they could easily watch the children and Mya spread the beach blanket while Evan pitched the beach umbrella. Evan brought a small cooler with drinks, although Mya did not pack a lunch. She and Evan decided that when it was time for lunch, they would leave the beach and head down the road to Andy's Drive-In. Jeffery most likely would want a hot dog, while his sister, just to be different would probably want a hamburger.

As Evan settled down in his beach chair, he looked across the cove, toward Buker Cottage. He could make out figures walking the grounds and checked his watch. "Matt Hamel is early in showing the property to his prospective clients today," he said to Mya.

"I hope it won't lead to anything," Mya replied, "otherwise, it might ruin 'The Plan.'"

"Speaking of which," said Evan, "do you realize that I don't have all the tools I need to carry out Matt's suggestions for our property?"

"What tools?" said Mya.

"He suggested cutting back the overgrown shrubs on the property line, but I don't have a hedge trimmer. He also thought we should cut down the dead maple tree in the back yard, but I don't have a chain saw."

"Does Brad have one?" she asked.

"He might, I'll call him later and ask."

"But he also suggested putting up additional shelving in the basement for storage," said Mya, "you have tools for that, don't you?"

"Yes," Evan replied, "and we also have paint brushes for the living room."

As Evan was turning his attention back to the children, Mya's cell phone went off. She checked the caller ID, activated the call, and said, "Hi Mom."

After a pause, she said, "Mom! I told you not to talk about it with anyone! I hope you didn't share what we talked about with anyone else in the family. . . . No! It's way too early for that! . . . No! That's crazy! He's going to drive four hours up here, and four hours back the same day? You can't let him do that! . . .Ugh! I don't like this idea at all, it's way too soon. . . I understand. Alright, he can come, but you and I need to discuss establishing some boundaries. . . . Yes. . . Alright, we'll talk tomorrow. Bye-bye."

As Mya hung up the phone, Evan said, "What was that all about?"

"I made the mistake of telling my mother about 'The Plan.' She told my father, and now he wants to come up here tomorrow with his business partner."

"What for?"

"He wants to look over the cottage so they can assess what needs to be done in order to winterize it and come up with a cost estimate."

"But that's very premature," said Evan.

"I know, I told her that, but he's insisting." After a pause, Mya continued, "You know, for years I watched him working for other people on construction projects. When he finally started his own contracting business, I was so proud and happy for him. Now, I just hope it's not a curse. I'm sorry. I should have kept my mouth shut."

"Don't worry about that," Evan replied. "Does he know how to winterize a cottage?"

"Mom says they winterized a couple of cottages in the Newport area. I guess they know what they're doing."

As Evan got up from his beach chair to walk over to the kids, he said, "I guess we'll find out!"

Chapter 17
The Inspection

The following day, Sunday, the Stuart family went to church as they normally do. When the service was over, Mya insisted on going to the supermarket before going to Buker Cottage. When they arrived at the cottage, Evan checked his watch. Mya's father and his partner would probably arrive within the hour.

"So much for painting the motorboat," Evan mused. He helped Mya unpack the grocery bags and said to her, "Let me get the kids settled while you start."

He kept the children busy while Mya prepared lunch, ham sandwiches for the children, and Portuguese codfish cakes for the adults. As she was finishing, a horn beeped outside, and Mya said, "They're here."

Speaking to the children, she said, "OK, everyone out on the deck so you can greet Avo and his friend."

The family walked out on to the deck, and after a few seconds Mya's father and his business partner emerged onto the deck as well. "Avo!" the children shouted in unison and ran to their grandfather to give him a hug.

"OOH, my Neto y Neta," said their grandfather as he hugged them back. He then turned his attention to his daughter and said, "Babla" as he embraced her and gave her a kiss on the cheek. He then looked over at his son-in law. "Evan!" he said shaking his hand.

"Alfonso," Evan replied, "how are you?"

"It's time you started calling me 'Al,'" he replied. Alfonso then gestured to the man next to him and said, "I would like you to meet Carlos, my partner."

"Pleased to meet you!" said Evan, as he shook hands with Carlos.

"Welcome!" added Mya. "Shall we go inside?"

Upon entering the cottage, Evan sat the children down in their places and proceeded to fill their cups with root beer.

"Root beer again!" exclaimed Jeffery. "Cool!"

The previous day, at Andy's Drive-In, the kids begged Evan and Mya to get them root beer, and Mya had picked up a large bottle at the supermarket when she picked up the other groceries earlier.

"Would you gentlemen like a beer?" Evan asked. "It's Corona. I know it's not your favorite, but I believe it's pretty good."

From the yearly family gatherings at the cottage, Evan knew that the favorite beer of the De la Rosa clan was a Portuguese beer known as Super Bock. Each year, Mya's cousins would bring a case of it to the gathering, and sometimes a case would not be enough.

"Sounds fine to me," said Carlos while Alfonso nodded. As Evan took out beers for them as Mya placed a platter of codfish cakes on the table, Carlos spoke again. "So, Evan, I noticed your boat when we came in. I'm partial to older boats. Can you tell me anything about it?"

"Well," replied Evan, "it's a 1950's era 16-foot White runabout. White is the brand name. It was built at the Old Town Canoe Company, right here in Maine."

"Interesting," replied Carlos. "What kind of motor does it have?"

"An Evinrude, 35 horsepower, they don't make them anymore."

"Evan was planning to paint it today," said Mya, "to get it ready for the water."

"That won't be a problem," said Alfonso. "We'll stay out of your way."

"Actually," responded Evan, "I'd like to hang out with you guys. Maybe I might learn a couple of things."

"That's fine with me," replied Alfonso while Carlos nodded.

After lunch, Evan followed Alfonso and Carlos out to their car. Alfonso took out a clipboard and measuring tape, while Carlos pulled out a small toolbox. They started taking measurements of the exterior of the cottage. Evan assisted Carlos in taking the measurements, while Alfonso took notes. Eventually, they came to the door to the utility room and opened it. The utility room couldn't be accessed from inside the cottage. It contained an electric water pump and holding tank for the well, an electric water heater, as well as fuse boxes and an electricity gauge.

"Hmmm," Alfonso began. "The insulation on these pipes is old. We're going to need to replace it with thicker insulation."

"And probably add a heating element," added Carlos. "Also, replace the fuse box with circuit brakers."

Alfonso made some notes and said, "We should think about putting a whole new walkway through here and adding a new doorway into the cottage." Alfonso turned to Evan and said, "We'll need it for the fire code."

"I see," replied Evan.

Carlos said, "Let's check the roof."

Evan took out the ladder, and Carlos climbed onto the roof. After examining the roof for a minute or two, he made his way back to the ladder and said, "I don't think it will need any spot repairs. It's old, but I think it has several good years left."

The men walked inside the cottage, again taking measurements, removing some wall panels and suspended ceiling tiles to estimate the amount of insulation that would be needed. After putting everything back in place, they went back outside and walked down to the lakeside front of the cottage. This time, Carlos spoke first, "Hmmm, at least it's raised high enough that we won't have to worry about hitting the water table, but I don't think the small excavator is going to work."

"You're right," added Alfonso. "They're going to have to dig this out by hand."

"Dig what out?" asked Evan.

"The cottage needs a basement," declared Alfonso. He turned toward the water and pointed his finger. "In the winter, when the temperature goes below freezing, the wind will come down off those mountains and across this frozen lake."

Turning back to Evan he continued, "That will make this cottage very cold and uncomfortable without a basement."

"We will need to install a heating system that can stand up to it," added Carlos. "In fact, we should consider moving everything from the utility room to the basement."

"Wow!" said Evan, realizing that this whole process was going to cost a lot more than he, Mya, and Matt Hamel thought it would.

Chapter18
"The Plan" Suffers a Setback

It was Monday evening. Evan was busy in the backyard trimming the shrubs, like Matt Hamel had suggested. Not having a hedge clipper of his own, Matt rented a battery operated one. Mya came out of the house with the kids, and they started to kick a ball around the yard. After a while, Mya left the children and walked over to Evan. "You realize, of course, that if Matt's plan is no longer viable, that all this work is for nothing."

"It's not for nothing," muttered Evan, "Regardless, these things need trimming."

"You're probably right," admitted Mya. "By the way, I asked Mrs. Turner to come and watch the children while we go and see Matt tomorrow. She said she'd be delighted."

"She's a good person," replied Evan. "We're fortunate to have her. So tell me again, what time is the meeting with Matt?"

"2pm."

"And you remember that I'm meeting with Ollie Iverson in the morning?"

"Yes,"

"Jeesh this is almost as busy as being in school."

Evan's Tuesday morning meeting with Ollie went well. It helped that Evan had already met with Mike, and they decided on a rotating schedule for Evan's general music classes. In the meantime, Ollie had negotiated a revised music schedule with the middle school principal, and in the end, they were able to craft workable teaching schedules for both of them. They agreed to meet again the following week to work on curriculum changes.

In the afternoon, Evan and Mya walked into Matt's office, to find that Matt was the only agent present. Everyone else had gone home. Matt's desk was almost completely devoid of papers, meaning this conference was probably his last agenda item of the day.

"How are you doing with my suggestions for your property?" Matt asked.

"We're working on it," Evan replied, "but I think we may have hit a snag."

Matt listened intently as Evan outlined what Alfonso and Carlos told him. After a few moments of thought, he said, "Well, they're correct about the heating system. The fireplace by itself would probably be ineffective during the winter. And I don't know if I could even argue with them about the basement. Without a basement, any exposed pipes below the floor of the bathroom and kitchen would be under constant threat of freezing."

"That kind of blows a hole in using our equity, doesn't it?" said Evan.

"A fatal one," said Matt. "Knowing what I know from the contractors around here, a good basement for the cottage could run as high as $100,000. It looks like my creative plan needs to be more creative."

As they headed home and Mya pulled into the driveway, she said, "OK, you send out Mrs. Turner, and I'll drive her home. But then I need to go shopping. Melanie's baby shower is tomorrow afternoon, and I still don't know what gift to get."

"You'll figure it out," said Evan as he opened the car door.

"You may have to start supper," said Mya.

"I think I'll make pancakes," said Evan. "The kids would love that."

"Don't you mess up my kitchen!"

Evan gave an impish smile and headed toward the house. As Mya sat in the car waiting for Mrs. Turner, her cell phone went off. She pulled out her phone, checked the caller ID, and activated the call.

"Hi Mom," she said.

"Hello Darling," replied her mother. "I called because I needed to ask you something. When is a good day that I can drive up and see you?"

"Not tomorrow, Mom," Mya answered. "It's going to be a busy day, and I'm trying to put a plan into place."

"What do you mean?" her mother asked.

"I've asked Evan to cut down a dead tree in the yard tomorrow. His friend Brad is going to come over to help him. That will free up Brad's wife, Melanie, so that we can throw a baby shower for her."

"Ooooh that sounds exciting!" said her mother.

"Anyway," continued Mya, "Thursday might work better. Evan will be painting the boat at the cottage and I'm staying home with the kids, so they won't be in his way."

"I see, do you think you can find something to keep the children occupied while I talk to you?"

Mya hesitated. "I guess I can Mom, but what's this all about? Why the big secret?"

"I can't tell you over the phone. There's a sensitive part to this, and I need to speak to you alone, without Evan and the children listening."

After a pause, Mya said, "Alright, I'll see you on Thursday."

Mya's plan on Wednesday went exactly as she had hoped. In the morning, Evan took the minivan down to the rental store. He returned the hedge clippers and rented a log splitter with wheels that the attendant hitched to the minivan. Just as Evan pulled into the driveway, Brad arrived at the house as well. The two went into the house and took some time to have coffee and blueberry muffins that Mya had prepared. Then it was time to get to work on the dead maple tree. Mya gathered the children, and all three watched from the window in Jeffery's bedroom.

"So, what do you say when you see the tree fall down?" she prompted them.

"Tim-Ber!" Jeff and Izzy shouted.

They turned their attention to Brad and Evan. Brad had taken a magic marker and drew on a section of the trunk for

Evan to "notch." The notch would lead the tree to fall in the direction that Brad intended it to, a clear spot in the yard where the tree wouldn't hit anything when it fell. Using Brad's chainsaw, Evan cut the notch where Brad had indicated, he started cutting through the trunk from the opposite side of the notch.

The tree fell exactly in the desired direction, and the children yelled "Tim-Ber!" as it hit the ground.

Evan and Brad spent the next couple of hours cutting the tree into logs. while Mya kept the children occupied indoors. After the tree had been cut into log size pieces, Evan drove the minivan with the log splitter attached up to the pile of logs and brought the children outside. He showed them where to start stacking the small size logs, and where to stand safely away from the log splitter as Brad and Evan ran the larger size logs from the trunk through it. Meanwhile, Mya snuck out in Evan's car to go to Melanie's baby shower.

As she drove off, Brad asked Evan, "What are you going to do with this wood again?"

"Well, tomorrow I'm going to rent a utility trailer, and the kids and I are going to load the logs on it and take them to the cottage for the fireplace. It was Mya's idea."

"You know, I could borrow my dad's pick-up and save you the cost of renting a trailer."

"Sounds great!" Evan replied.

"And then," Brad continued, "once the wood is seasoned, Buker cottage will have an ample supply of wood for its fireplace. A splendid degree of foresight Margo-sub, errr, sorry."

"Sorry? That sounds like progress. Did you talk with Lisa?"

"Actually, she sent me to talk with Samantha Wilson at the high school. Apparently, she has more experience with grief issues."

"Well," said Evan, "I'm proud of you."

Chapter 19
An Unexpected Gift

Mya put the coffee on in preparation for her mother's arrival. Evan had gone to the rental store earlier to return the log splitter. As he arrived home, Brad drove in behind him with his father's pick-up. Then, along with the kids, they spent the next hour and a half loading the vehicle with logs from the cut-down maple tree. They made one trip to the cottage to unload the majority of the logs, and then returned to load the rest. Mya insisted that Brad stay for lunch before they made the second trip to the cottage. She told Evan about her mother's visit, and asked Evan to take the children in the minivan and keep them at the cottage until she called to tell him that her mother had left. She left out the part about her mother also not wanting Evan within earshot. Mya's mom arrived not more than ten minutes after Evan left with the kids for the cottage. When she arrived, Mya served coffee and blueberry muffins left over from yesterday.

"OK Mom, what's this all about?"

"Your father and I have been talking the last few days, and we've made a decision."

"That sounds ominous," replied Mya, "What kind of decision?" Mya's mother, Gabriella De la Rosa, was almost always a picture of sophistication. But at this moment, she looked embarrassed and confused as she struggled for words. "It's not ominous. It's a good thing. But you know, when you started dating Evan, your father and I were very disappointed."

"Mom."

"Let me finish!" Gabriella interrupted. "When the two of you decided to get married, I was beside myself. I knew of a couple of Portuguese boys, sons of people we know, good families, who I thought would make a good match for you. Your father was disappointed as well, and we were convinced that your marriage to Evan wouldn't last. Evan was from California. He was unfamiliar with our ways and traditions. That's why for your wedding, we gave you, what I'm embarrassed to say, was very much a token gift."

"Mom, the gift..."

"Stop!" ordered Gabriella. After a pause, she continued. "But we were wrong. Evan has turned out to be a devoted husband, a wonderful father, a responsible and thoughtful man. In many ways, the two of you get along better than your father and I have through the years."

"That's very kind of you to say Mom."

"It's true," Gabriella continued. "Even beyond that, he has accepted us, accepted the whole family. He has embraced our traditions, and now, we can't imagine him not being part of the family. That's why your father and I have decided to make up for that disgraceful wedding gift."

"You don't have to do that mom."

"We think that we do," Mya's mother replied. "We've decided to give you and Evan something valuable toward the winterization of the cottage. We no longer have any children living at home, and your father's business is doing very well. We can afford it."

"What kind of value are we talking about?" Gabriella rose from her chair and said, "We're not sure of the dollar amount, but we're going to underwrite the cost of the basement."

"Mom! we can't possibly accept that! That's like a hundred thousand dollars!"

"No, it won't cost that much. First of all, your father considers the hundred thousand dollar estimate to be way too high. Plus, he believes he can wheel and deal with the contractors around here. And once the foundation is poured, he feels he can bring his own crew up here to finish the basement off."

"That's still thousands and thousands of dollars," argued Mya, We just can't accept a gift like that!" Mya's mother walked toward her daughter with a facial expression that Mya was well familiar with, the one that communicated.

"I'm laying down the law," her mother said in a very matter-of-fact tone. "You can, and we insist. Whatever the cost finally ends up being, the happiness of you and your family is worth ten times that much."

Mya was at a loss for words. She jumped out of her chair to hug her mother. The two women embraced, both in tears. After her mother had left, Mya called her husband to say it was time to bring the kids home. She then called Matt Hamel and told him, "There's been a new development in 'The Plan.'"

Matt Hamel was in his office, preparing to go home for the day. Just as he was ready to leave the phone rang. He picked up the receiver and said, "Hamel Real Estate, this is Matt,"

"Hello Matt," said the voice at the other end. "This is Amy Buker, returning your call."

Matt said, "Well, thank you for getting back to me. Do you have time to talk?"

"We do," said Amy. "I'm on my lunch break right now, but I'm also the boss, so we have all the time we need. What's up?"

"Well, do you remember when we were talking, and you said you would prefer to sell the cottage to Evan and Mya rather than strangers?"

"Yes, I remember."

"What if I were to tell you that I've devised a way for them to make that happen?"

"I can't imagine how you could have done that, but if it's true I would be very pleased."

"Well, I have to tell you, it's a crazy plan, with some unusual components. It would require some generosity on your part, as well as your trust that some of the crazier steps will work, but if Evan and Mya agree to some of the demanding components on their end, I think they can purchase it from you for $300,000."

"That's somewhat lower than your original estimate, but it's still pretty good," replied Amy.

"Well, that's the generosity part," said Matt.

Amy understood.

"Tell me more about these crazy steps."

"Well, to begin with, you would not be getting the money immediately. You would be selling the cottage to them through a lease-purchase agreement."

"I've heard of those," said Amy, "but I don't know a lot about them."

"Well, Evan and Mya would pay for the cottage by sending you a monthly payment. But essentially, instead of them getting a mortgage from the bank they would be getting a mortgage from you."

After a pause, Amy said, "Wait, If I'm holding a mortgage for them, by the time they pay it off in 30 years, I'll be almost 90."

"No, No, No," replied Matt, "this wouldn't be a 30-year mortgage. They would pay off the mortgage in 15 years."

"15 years?" said Amy thoughtfully. "I think I might be able to live with that."

"Of course," Matt continued, "they wouldn't start making payments to you until they sell the house they currently live in."

"Why would they do that?"

Matt went on to explain the need for the Stewarts to sell their house which would allow them to use the equity in the home to winterize the cottage.

"That's an excellent idea," said Amy.

"Thank you for saying that," replied Matt. "But the reason the sale price is three hundred thousand is because that's the maximum mortgage payment that they can afford, and even with that, Mya will need to agree to get a job so both of them would be working."

"Hmm, That's certainly a sacrifice on her part. I guess we'll see what she decides," said Amy. "When do you plan to talk to them?"

"When their house goes on the market," replied Matt. "So it may be a few weeks before I send you a contract. Plus, I have one other surprise suggestion for them."

Chapter 20
The Sacrifice Becomes Apparent

Mya emerged from the basement, followed by Matt Hamel and Evan. She called to her children, playing in the backyard, and everybody went into the house. She sat the children down in the newly painted living room and put on their favorite cartoon video. She then followed the men into the kitchen and poured coffee for everyone.

"Well, you've both done a wonderful job," Matt said as he poured sugar into his coffee. "The property looks great; The shelving in the basement is outstanding; Mya, not only did you do a great job painting the living room, but you've managed to get the children to keep their rooms so tidy, how do you do it?"

Mya smiled as she sat down at the table. "They're just great kids, I guess."

"Well," Matt continued, "I think we can put this house on the market whenever you're ready, although there are some things about 'The Plan' that we probably should discuss."

"What things?" asked Evan.

"Well, for one thing, I've had a couple of phone conversations with Amy. I explained the 'The Plan' to her, and she finds it acceptable. She's willing to go along with a lease-purchase agreement, although..." and Matt started chuckling. "She wanted me to write a contingency clause into the contract. She wanted to make the sale contingent on you bringing the kids to San Francisco for a visit before summer vacation ends."

Evan laughed. "I think we can do that. It sounds great!"

"Well, it's not that great," replied Matt, suddenly becoming serious.

As Evan and Mya gave him questioning looks, Matt said, "Amy was very generous when she agreed to drop the selling price from $350,000 to $300,000. However, I don't think she would be willing to drop it any further, nor would I be inclined to think that she should, given the situation of needing to take care of your father. But Mya, when you were asking about the sacrifice part, this is where that factor comes in. Now, don't get me wrong, the willingness of your parents to cover the cost of the basement is nothing short of extraordinary. It's really wonderful, and it's a critical component to pushing this crazy idea over the top. However, the bottom line is that the two of you would be carrying a $300,000 mortgage, and the mortgage payment for that would be more than twice the amount that you're currently paying on this house."

"How much?" asked Mya, dreading the answer to follow. "Two thousand dollars a month, and that's with Amy being generous again in accepting a very low interest rate. I certainly would love to see this plan come to fruition, but you cannot float a mortgage payment of this size on Evan's income alone."

"So, I'll need to go to work, get a job," said Mya. "That IS a sacrifice!"

Evan walked Matt out to his car as he prepared to leave. He then returned to the kitchen to find Mya sitting at the table, tears streaming down her face.

Evan hugged his wife and said, "Look, we don't have to do this. We haven't made any financial commitment at this point. We can pull out of this project, and it will not have cost us anything except a few hours doing major jobs around the house that probably should have been done anyway."

"You're right," said Mya, "but think of the alternative, giving up the cottage, denying the children the opportunity to grow up on the water, denying you, us, the chance to grow old with the lake as our companion."

After a pause, she said, "I don't think I can live with that."

For a minute or so, no one said anything.

Then Mya said, "I suppose I could check down on Main St. and see if any of those places are hiring."

"That won't work," said Evan. "As he was leaving, Matt told me that you needed to find a professional job with an income similar to mine. A minimum wage job down on Main St. isn't going to cut it."

"I have a B. A. from Wellesley! That should count for something."

"If it does, I'm not exactly sure what," replied Evan. "Mya, you were a music major. It's not quite the same thing as having a medical or engineering degree."

"Well, what about teaching?" said Mya. "I'm not as good as you, but I think I can do OK."

"I'm certain you can," replied Evan, "but you're not state certified. That makes finding a teaching job very difficult. You might be able to find an elementary school willing to take a chance on you, but it would mean obtaining emergency temporary certification from the state. You would then have three years to earn the needed college credits to become fully certified. The only places you could go for that are UMaine or Portland, and it would mean driving 90 minutes down there, a three-hour class, followed by a 90-minute trip home, all while trying to juggle a full-time job. I'm certainly willing to take up the slack with the kids and the household, but I can't help thinking it would take a tremendous toll on you."

"Maybe," replied Mya, "but let's not rule it out. Let's take a few days to research this and see where it leads."

"I'm fine with that," said Evan as he hugged Mya again and said, "However this turns out, we'll face it together."

Mya hugged her husband back and said, "Agreed."

Chapter 21
A Promising Development

Ollie Iverson sipped his coffee as he studied the revised curricular expectations draft for music in the middle school that Evan had prepared.

"Whoa! Dude! This stuff is good!" Ollie said to Evan. "Man, you have a gift for writing all this educational jargon."

"Thanks," replied Evan, "but what I don't understand is how you were able to convince Helen to change around the middle school schedule to accommodate us."

Ollie sat back in his chair in thought. The way he worded his answer could end up being a teachable moment from a veteran music teacher like himself with many years' experience, to a young teacher, such as Evan, who was still learning the finer points of the craft.

"It's like this dude," Ollie began, "Helen Barker is the kind of principal that has a hard time seeing the bigger picture beyond her own school. Knowing that such a myopic viewpoint was her bag, I was able to convince her that having us run the music program the way Barbara did, along with our teaching responsibilities at the other schools just wasn't practical. Plus, I played the 'tough' card."

"The 'tough' card?"

"That you and I could have been real hard asses, and said 'Helen, it was your school that suffered the music teacher cut, so tough bongos to you,' but no, because of our professional sensibilities, we decided to pitch in and secure a sequential program of study in music throughout all the grades, and thereby not leave the middle school hanging."

"Well," said Evan, "I'm glad you were so convincing."

"Of course, that wasn't the strategy I used on the superintendent."

"What do you mean?" asked Evan.

Imitating the voice from one of his favorite movies, Ollie said, "You see Grasshopper, as superintendent, Eric sees the big picture, so for him, the tough card would have been wasted. Sooo, with him, I had to play the 'hurt' card."

"What's that?"

"Well, you know man, there's a lot of teachers that believe that when cuts happen, the best approach is to make them hurt in the community. If we cut my music history class, a few students will be disappointed, but it doesn't cause much harm to the community. If we go in front of the Lakeport Athletic Boosters Club and say, 'Sorry folks, but because of budget cuts, the band won't be able to perform at football games this year,' that hurts, and it tends to reflect badly on the superintendent and school board."

"I never thought of it that way," said Evan.

"One day," Ollie said, using his best sage voice, "you will learn this for yourself, Grasshopper!"

After Evan left the meeting with Ollie, he made a quick stop at the elementary school. He found Mike in his office and said, "Hey Mike, do you have a minute?"

"Of course," said Mike as he pushed his chair away from his desk and gestured to Evan to take a seat.

"What's up?"

"Actually, it's a personal favor. Would it be possible to move Brad's 5th grade music class, and Marion Craft's 1st grade music class to the end of the day?"

"Yeah, I don't think that would be a problem," replied Mike, "but why?"

Mike listened intently as Evan explained the need for Mya to find a job, and that at this point he had no idea what form that job would take. If his last music class of the day took place in the elementary school, as opposed to the middle school, then there would not be any need to bus Jeffery to day care after school. He could come to Evan's classroom, and they could leave school together.

"I'm sure we can set that up," said Mike, "but tell me, what kind of job is Mya considering?"

Evan went on to explain Mya's background and experience, and when he finished, Mike said, "You know, I might be able to help with this. There's a golfing buddy of mine. His name is Arnie Pulaski and he's the principal of Hillerston Elementary school. He has a music teacher opening at his school, in fact, if we had actually lost you, the first thing I would have done is call Arnie about you. To my knowledge, he hasn't filled the vacancy yet. In fact, I think he's having difficulties filling it, and I would have no problem talking him and suggesting he have a talk with Mya."

"That would be wonderful," said Evan.

"Well, not that wonderful," replied Mike. "Mya needs to understand that if she were to be offered this position and accept it, she would be taking a risk."

"What do you mean?" asked Evan.

"I'm not sure of the details," replied Mike, "but three years ago, the music teacher there got into a big argument with the school board. The board forced out the music teacher by reducing his hours to one day a week."

"One day a week? You can't possibly teach a program with a time limitation like that."

"Correct, which is why the teacher left. So for the last three years, the program has struggled, and finally Arnie decided enough was enough, and convinced the school board to restore the position to full time. However, in the interim, it appears that word spread among the music education community, and now it seems that no veteran music teacher will touch the position with a ten foot pole."

"Really," said Evan, "I can see why. I heard that the program there was struggling, but I wasn't aware of the full story."

"Well, Mya needs to understand that if she were to take that position, there would be no guaranties."

"I'll certainly tell her," Evan replied, "although I've never seen her back down from a challenge. In fact, I believe she would be totally determined to succeed in a situation like that."

"Okay then," said Mike, "let's proceed on that assumption. As it turns out, I'm playing golf with Arnie tomorrow. I'll talk to him about it then."

As Evan walked into the house, he could feel the anticipation. Today was "move-in" day, when the family would make the move to Buker Cottage, well, at least until summer vacation ended. As he approached the kitchen, he could hear Mya on the phone.

"No Amy, I think that would be fine, and yes, we're looking forward to it. . . . Alright, I'll give you a call once the travel arrangements are made, OK?. . . fine. . . you too, bye-bye."

She turned to Evan after disconnecting the call. "I'm sure you're aware," she said to Evan, "that your old room is now a guest room in their house, and that's where we'll be staying."

"Yes, I'm aware of that. What about the kids?"

"They're going to sleep on cots in the TV room. She thinks they'll enjoy that."

"I'm sure they will. Let's hope that you don't get a call for an interview when we're out there."

"What do you mean?" asked Mya. Evan went on to explain about the music teacher opening in Hillerston, and Mya's eyes widened.

"You realize," said Evan "if you were to be offered this position, you could be walking into a hornets nest."

"I understand," replied Mya, "I'll just have to prepare for it all the harder, assuming I can get your help on this."

"You'll have it," said Evan.

Chapter 22
The Rest of Matt's Plan

att Hamel was looking through his folder trying to find a particular sheet of paper. Mya and Evan waited patiently while he searched.

"I know it's here somewhere," Matt said as he continued to shuffle papers, "Okay, here it is," he finally said. "Now, Amy understands that in order to move forward, your house would need to be sold. So, I've written into the contract that the sale of the cottage is contingent upon the sale of your house."

"That sounds correct," said Evan.

"Now there's one issue that we need to focus on today regarding the sale of your property."

"Our property?" asked Mya

"Yes, I was reviewing your original mortgage document, and I did some recalculating. It seems the amount of equity that we originally discussed was not correct."

"No?" asked Evan.

"Well," Matt continued, "I was under the impression that you've only owned that property for five years."

"No," said Evan we bought it seven years ago."

"I know that now," replied Matt, "so when I discovered my error, I did some recalculating of the equity. It turns out that the equity in your property isn't $30,000, it's almost $37.000."

"Really?" said Mya.

"Yes, now, you may remember that when we talked about selling your property, that you told me that you would want to delay the closing of your property until the winterization of the cottage was completed."

"That's correct," said Evan, "It only made sense."

"Perhaps at that time it made sense, but now, I'd like to make another suggestion. The idea of staying in your house while the winterization is completed, and delaying the closing of the property makes it more difficult to sell the property. Many prospective buyers are turned off at the idea that the closing would be delayed for several months. When we find a buyer and put the house under contract, I'm suggesting a normal amount of time to close the sale, about 8-10 weeks."

"So, what would we do in the meantime?" asked Mya.

"Look," said Matt, "with your parents covering the cost of the basement, your equity would easily cover the insulation of the cottage, the new entrance by the kitchen that you would need for the fire code, and installation of drywall to create rooms in the basement. In fact, you may want to think about setting up the children's rooms in the basement. It will probably be warmer than the bedrooms in the loft."

"I understand what you're saying," said Mya, "but what about my original question. What do we do while the renovations to the cottage are taking place?"

"My point is that you don't need the extra equity that I discovered for the winterization," Matt continued. "I'm suggesting you use it to rent an apartment while the renovations are underway."

"An apartment," Evan repeated, with a very unsure voice.

"You may or may not be aware," Matt continued "a decent apartment in this area with, say, two bedrooms, rents for about one thousand dollars a month. Your extra equity would cover that easily."

"Two bedrooms?" asked Mya.

"Well, the kids might have to share a room for a few months."

"I would prefer a three bedroom," said Mya. "That wouldn't break the bank. would it?"

"I don't think it would," replied Matt, "but there aren't a whole lot of three-bedroom rentals around here. You may need to be prepared for the possibility that a three-bedroom may not be available."

"I see," said Evan

"You know," Matt continued, "we also do apartment rentals out of this office. I'll ask our rental person to be on the lookout for three-bedroom units."

"Hopefully, it will work," said Evan.

"Well then," Matt said, "let's get the paperwork done and get your property on the market. I'll be by later this afternoon to put up a FOR SALE sign."

"I probably should take photos to commemorate the event," said Evan.

"Well, I won't be there," said Mya, "I have an interview this afternoon."

In fact, the interview was all Mya could talk about on the ride home. "What if he asks me about classroom discipline?"

"It's true that you've only worked with adults in the choir," said Evan, "but I've seen instances where you've had to lay down the law in order to maintain the choir's attention. In some ways, attention is more intrinsic in music class than, say, an English class. Just remember the three-step process we discussed for dealing with an unruly student."

"First incident," said Mya, "verbal warning or conference with the student. Second incident, isolate the student in a corner of the classroom. Third incident, contact the office and send out the student."

"I think you'll do fine," said Evan.

"What if he's not really considering me?"

"Sweetie, we've sent him your letter of application, the resume we drew up highlighting your music experience, and you arranged for Wellesley to send him a transcript. Plus, I'm sure Mike spoke positively to him about you, and that should count for a lot. I'm sure if he wasn't interested, he wouldn't be seeing you."

"I hope you're right," said Mya. "By the way, make sure that the fish Jeff caught is cleaned by the time I get home."

"I promise, it will be done," Evan replied.

The previous afternoon, Jeff had been out with Evan fishing. Having had his fill of fishing with worms, Jeff wanted to fish using a fishing lure on his pole like his father. It was a very warm day with temperatures in the 90's, unusual for Maine, but Evan wanted to indulge in his son's request and actually gave him Gordon's lucky lure to use, the one that Gordon had used to catch the large bass that he had mounted and placed on the "archive wall." Jeff hadn't had any luck, and eventually it was time to head back to the cottage for supper. Evan turned aside Jeff's pleading to stay longer, and instead suggested a compromise. They would troll back to the cottage. Jeff cast his line off the stern of the boat, while Evan guided the motorboat back to the cottage at a very slow speed. As this plan proceeded, they passed a raft just offshore from one of the cottages. A few seconds later, Jeffery's line went taught, and the force was enough to almost pull his child's fishing pole out of his hands.

Excitedly, Jeff shouted, "Daddy! Daddy!"

Evan turned around and saw Jeff's tiny fishing pole bending so that the normally straight fishing pole formed a 'C.'

Something big was on the line. It must have been under the raft to stay out of the sun, Evan realized. "Let me have the pole to reel him in," he instructed his Jeffery.

Evan took his son's pole and felt the pull on it. The test strength of the line on Jeffery's pole was considerably less than the line on his adult pole, and Evan worried that the line might break. Slowly and patiently, he nursed the fish closer and closer. When he finally managed to get the fish close enough to the boat, he used his fishing net and managed to snag it. It was a bass, not as big as the one that Gordon had caught, but a good size one, nonetheless.

Wide eyed, Jeffery shouted, "C'mon Dad, we have to get back to the cottage so I can show Mom and Izzy."

Evan kicked the outboard motor into high speed, and in no time, they were pulling up to the dock at Buker Cottage. As soon as he was able, Jeff jumped off the motorboat onto the dock. Still wearing his life jacket, and fish in hand, he ran up to the cottage. As Evan secured to motorboat to the dock, he could hear Mya's raised voice through the open windows saying to Jeff, "Don't you bring that thing in here young man! Take it outside right now!"

As Evan neared the door, he could see the rest of his family just outside the cottage, Jeffery proudly showing off the fish to his mother and sister. At the request of her son, she took out her cell phone to take a picture of Jeffery holding his catch.

"Mom," he said, "could we please have this for supper tonight?"

"I'm not eating that!" said Izzy.

"We can't have it tonight," said his mother, "I already have supper ready for tonight," she said, "besides, I'm not cleaning that thing!"

Evan then spoke up, "I would suggest we wrap it and put it in the refrigerator. Tomorrow, I'll show Jeff how to clean it, and we can serve it tomorrow night."

Now, as the car was pulling up to the cottage, Evan reassured his wife once again that he and Jeff would start cleaning the fish as soon as they could. Isabel probably would not touch it at supper, but Evan was relatively certain that Jeffery would.

Chapter 23
The Dominos Start Falling

Could the penny actually have worked? Maybe, maybe not, but it certainly appeared to be good fortune. Evan found an errant penny in the bathroom that morning. At first, he thought it must have been Izzy playing with her piggy bank again, but then he realized that Izzy's piggy bank was back at their house, not the cottage. As lunch time approached, he received a call from Matt Hamel. Evan had to pull the phone from his ear, because Matt was practically shouting on the other end.

"Six days! Can you believe it? Six days! I mean, I've moved property fast before, but this? It may be a record! I should go back and check!" It had been six days since the Stuart residence was placed on the market. That very morning, Matt had shown the property to a young couple. The couple appeared quite taken by the property and told Matt they wished to make an offer. They went to Matt's office, and Matt filled out the paperwork.

After the couple left, Matt called Evan with the offer. At this point, Matt had calmed down a bit, and said, "As I'm sure you know, you're free to accept or decline the offer, especially when you consider that their bid is Two thousand dollars less than your asking price. Plus, they want to do a VA mortgage which means there will be some extra hoops we need to jump through."

"I don't want to spend any time haggling," said Evan, "let's accept the offer and get moving with the rest of 'The Plan.'"

"Alright," said Matt. "Your property is officially now under contract. As far as 'The Plan' goes, all we need to do now is draw up the lease-purchase agreement for Amy to sign, and work can start on the basement."

"I'll look forward to that," said Evan, "but won't we need to move out of the cottage once they start working on it?"

"Not at first," replied Matt, "but at some point, work on the basement will make the foundation too delicate for anyone to occupy the cottage. By that time, I hope to see you moved into an apartment."

"I see," said Evan.

"So," continued Matt, "if you wish, you and Mya can come down to the office this afternoon, you can sign the lease purchase agreement, and I can fax it to Amy for her signature."

"Uuhn, not today," replied Evan. "Mya isn't here. She went to the State Education Office in Augusta to apply for emergency teacher certification."

"Really?" said Matt.

"That's right," continued Evan. "The next time you see her, she will officially be the new music teacher at Hillerston Elementary School."

"Excellent!" Matt exclaimed.

"Besides," Evan continued, "instead of faxing the agreement to Amy, we would like you to allow us to take the agreement with us to California next week so that we can present it to her personally."

Mya walked down the corridor of the nursing home conversing with Amy, while the rest of the family trailed behind. "It's twelve courses in all," Mya was saying. "It's going to take all three years to complete, but the good news is that many of them can be completed online."

"That sounds great," said Amy,

"That's not all," continued Mya. "One of the professors has agreed to teach her course as an independent study over the internet. It turns out she's a mother with young children also, so it works for both of us. Granted, there are some courses, like the Technology in Education course that I'll have to drive down to Portland for, but at least I won't have to make the trip twice a week for three years."

At that point the group walked into Carlton's room. Before leaving for the nursing home, Mya had tried to prepare the children for the visit, taking special care to explain it to Izzy.

"Now listen," she said to her daughter. "Grampa is like Avo, except that he is daddy's father."

"Daddy's father?" echoed Izzy, trying to process the idea.

"That's right," continued Mya, "But Grampa has a big, big, boo-boo. The boo-boo is so bad that Grampa can't walk or talk."

"He can't?" Isabel was obviously having a difficult time imagining this scenario.

"No," continued Mya, "so when you go on his bed, make sure you give him the biggest hug you can, but remember that he cannot hug you back, because he can't move his arms."

"Oh," replied Izzy, "ok."

Mya smiled. The one thing she loved most about her daughter was that in the end, Izzy always seemed to defer to being agreeable.

Upon entering Carlton's room, Evan walked over and hugged his father.

"Hi Dad!" he said. "Your grandchildren are here. This is Jeffery, and Isabel."

As if on cue, the children climbed onto Carlton's bed to give him a big hug. Carlton couldn't move, but his facial expression reflected pure joy and gratitude. Mya couldn't be sure, but it looked like he might be fighting back tears. Mya walked over to the bed and proceeded to help Izzy get down and stand next to the bed.

She then leaned over and gave Carlton a kiss on the cheek and said, "Hi Dad!"

Carlton tapped on the pad of paper under his hand, and Amy immediately inserted a pencil in Carlton's left hand. Carlton started writing, with Amy, now experienced at this task, moving the pad of paper as necessary. When he had finished, Amy showed the pad to everyone.

"Jeffery, can you read what Grampa wrote?" Evan asked.

"It says," Jeff replied, squinting at the pad, trying to sound out the letters. "HHHHI ALL."

"Very good!" Amy said as she clapped her hands. "Why don't you tell Grampa what grade you're going into when school starts."

"I'm gonna be in first grade!" Jeffery announced proudly.

Not to be outdone, Izzy chimed in. "And I'm...I'm gonna go to Miss Audrey's nursey school!"

"Nursery school," Mya corrected.

Carlton tapped his left hand, and tearing off the top sheet, Amy immediately placed the pad under her husband's hand, as well as replacing the pencil. This time, when Carlton finished, Amy held up the pad and showed Jeffery. "GRRREEEE, I'm not sure."

"It says 'Great'" Evan told his son.

"I know," he said, "that's a hard one."

The visit went on, with the children telling their grandfather all about being at the lake. When Jeffery told him that he had caught his first fish, Carlton smiled. Mya went on to tell her father-in-law about her new teaching position, and how Evan was helping her prepare. Amy then relayed what the therapists were telling her, that Carlton was making great progress, and that he might be able to go home at some point.

"We'll be able to arrange for homecare," Amy said. "It will certainly be more affordable than the nursing home."

"Probably better food too," said Mya, "Speaking of which," she put her hand on Carlton's shoulder. "How would you like me to make Peri Peri chicken, and we can bring some over to you?"

Carlton's eyes lit up, and he blinked twice.

"That means 'Yes.'" Amy told the children.

Just after Jeffery was born, Carlton travelled to Maine for a visit. Amy couldn't make the trip due to work commitments, but during his visit, Mya made Peri Peri chicken, and Carlton fell in love with it. As they were preparing to leave, Carlton tapped on his pad once more. When he finished writing, Amy showed the Pad to Evan. It read "PROUD."

"Thanks Dad," Evan said as he fought tears of his own, and as everyone turned to leave, he added, "We'll be back tomorrow."

Chapter 24
"The Plan" is Fulfilled

The children were watching TV while the adults were seated at Amy's dining room table.

"I'm happy to do this," Amy said as she signed the lease-purchase agreement that Evan had brought. "I feel so much better turning the cottage over to you, as opposed to strangers."

"Well, we're very grateful," said Mya. "I can't even begin to tell you what it means to us. The chance for the children to grow up on the lake, the chance for Evan and me to spend the rest of our years there, it's just priceless."

"Not to mention the De la Rosa family gathering?" Amy said, a touch of mischief creeping into her voice.

"Well," said Mya, "my parents have already suggested to us to hold a celebration event. I've been discouraging it. I need to concentrate on preparing for my teaching position when the school year starts. I really don't have time for all the planning and preparation, but my parents are insisting."

"You have to decide what's best for you," said Amy. "I'm sure the event will be all the much sweeter next year, when you can celebrate it with the renovations to the cottage completed."

"Matt Hamel told us that you were very generous in the terms of the agreement. That's so magnanimous of you in light of the need to take care of Carlton."

"Well," said Amy, "the accountant and the elder attorney finally seem to be ironing things out, and it looks like the path forward is slowly coming into focus."

"I'm glad to hear it," said Mya.

"Besides," continued Amy, "seeing the sacrifice that you two needed to make for this to work? Well, I just couldn't stand by and let 'The Plan' fall by the wayside. I feel bad that you have to go to work in order to make the mortgage payments."

"It's worth it," replied Mya. "Fortunately, Miss Audrey's Nursery School also doubles as a day care center. The plan is that when Evan and Jeffery leave school at the end of the day, they will swing by Miss Audrey's to pick up Izzy."

"I see, so that means you will need to be driving Evan's car?"

"I guess, at least at first. The grand plan is that at some point, we will trade in Evan's car for a 4-door pick-up truck with a snowplow attachment."

"What? Why?"

"Well, once we move into the cottage full time, we'll be the only year-round residents of that dirt road. The town won't plow the dirt road, so it's up to us."

"My goodness, I hadn't thought of that," said Amy "What other adjustments will you need to make?"

"Trash disposal," Evan interjected. "Our current house is located within the urban area zone of the town, so our trash gets picked up by the town every week, but the outskirts of the town, where the lake is located isn't within the zone, so there's no trash pick-up there."

"But when I was at the lake, I remember the trash being picked up," said Amy.

"That was an independent trash refuse company," replied Evan. "That service is still available. Lake residents pay the company to pick up their trash in the summertime, but that service isn't available in the off-season, so I'll need to make a weekly run to the town transfer station to dispose of our trash."

At that point, the children entered the dining room. "We don't wanna watch TV," said Izzy.

"Yeah," Jeff added. "There's nothing on, it's all grown-up stuff."

"I know exactly what to do," said Amy as she grabbed her laptop. "We're going to plan the things we're going to do tomorrow. Come here, look at this!" she said as she punched up the visual of a cable car. "I'll bet you've never taken a ride on a cable car."

"It looks cool," said Jeff.

"Yeah, cool," agreed Izzy, not completely understanding the conversation. Amy went on in an animated fashion, "There's a very nice playground in Golden Gate Park, and of course we have to ride the carousel. We should also consider seeing the Bison that they have there. I remember reading that Bison are very rare in Maine...."

As Amy continued to plan with the children, Evan and Mya quietly went into the kitchen.

"I should start on dinner," Mya said as she opened the refrigerator. "The peri peri chicken isn't going to make itself."

"I'm glad you decided to go with chicken fingers," said Evan, "that will make it easier to cut up into small pieces for dad."

"That was the plan," said Mya as she reached for the bag of groceries, she had purchased on the way back from the nursing home. "You do realize you're going to have to make this for him every time we visit."

"I don't mind," replied Mya. "I'm guessing there aren't a lot of things he can enjoy these days. If I can do my own little part to provide him with a little bit of enjoyment, that'll be just fine."

"It's gonna be great. Do you need help?" asked Evan.

"Maybe, I'll let you know. For now, why don't you go back to the dining room, and make sure Amy doesn't have us running all over creation tomorrow."

Chapter 25
Six years later

Evan and Mya cheered loudly along with all the other people on the deck of the clubhouse. The Evergreen Lake Yacht Club was holding its annual swim meet, and 12-year-old Jeffery was in the middle of racing in the breaststroke event. The swim meet had to be cancelled during the COVID years, but now it seemed as if there was never an interruption. It was Jeffery's second year competing in the junior division, 11–14-year-olds. The previous year, Jeff had competed in a couple of events. He didn't do very well, but after his initial disappointment, he developed a determination to succeed. This year, in the weeks prior to the swim meet, Jeffery, with the guidance of Evan, embarked upon a training regimen for the competition. Each day, Jeff would swim laps from the dock to the raft that Evan and Mya recently purchased which sat in the water about 40 feet from the dock. At first, it was just freestyle, but then Evan taught Jeffery the breaststroke and Jeff started doing breaststroke laps as well. It seemed to be paying off, as Jeff finished the 100-foot course for second place.

"Good job Jeffery!" Mya yelled.

"He deserves it," said Evan, "he worked hard."

His red second place ribbon would go along with his blue first place ribbon for the freestyle that he won earlier. Evan would add them to the newly restored archive wall in the cottage. As he stood on the clubhouse deck, Evan looked over to the beach area. Once the junior division competition concluded, the activity would shift to the beach, where the small-fry races would be held. The small-fry races, one for boys and one for girls would be held in waist deep water. The

8–10-year-old swimmers would race parallel to the shore for about 50 feet. This would be Izzy's first year competing as the 9-year-old had just spent this summer learning to swim without her "swimmies" buoyancy aids. Evan glanced to the other side of the clubhouse, where the marina stood. The marina consisted of three 50-foot docks, with boat slips attached. Although the yacht club owned an impressive clubhouse with a large deck and good size ballroom which sometimes hosted wedding receptions, calling the organization a "yacht club" was a bit of a stretch. With the exception of a half-dozen or so sailboats, the remainder of the boat slips contained motorboats and pontoon boats. There was nothing in the marina that one could classify as a yacht. Evan turned his attention back to the meet. The underwater challenge was getting underway.

"How do you think he'll do?" asked Mya,

"I don't know," replied Evan, "he didn't prepare for this like he did the other events."

The whistle blew, and the contestants all dove into the water together and swam underwater for as long as they could before needing to come up for air. After about 30 seconds, heads started popping up in various places. When Jeff broke the surface, it looked as though he had gone the fifth farthest distance. No ribbon this time for Jeff.

"Next year, we'll see," mused Evan.

"Okay Izzy," said Mya, "come with me and I'll take you down to where your race is going to be."

Izzy took her mother's hand, and they went off.

Evan took in his surroundings. "A great day," he said to himself softly, "no whitecaps."

Looking across the bay, Evan could see that the cooler August nights were having their effect. The leaves on some of the trees had actually started to turn colors. In another month, the leaves would start changing in earnest, and school will have started. Evan's thoughts turned toward the new school year. Mya was well established and well liked in her position at Hillerston Elementary. Evan had been back at Lakeport

Elementary School full time for four years now. After teaching in both the elementary school and middle school for a couple of years, he and Ollie finally convinced the schoolboard to restore the lost middle school music position. They hired a young woman out of college named Maggie Grover. She was originally from New Zealand and had a charming Kiwi accent. Evan felt that she fit in quite well in the middle school.

The rest of the summer was pretty much planned out. On Tuesday, the family would head to Logan Airport to catch a flight for their annual summer trip to California, spending a few days visiting Carlton and Amy. Carlton had made steady progress over the years. He was now living at home and receiving homecare as needed. He was talking now, although his speech was slurred, and he was now able to sit in a wheelchair. To be able to talk with his grandchildren was something Carlton treasured. After the California trip, there would be shopping in earnest for clothes for the new school year, which the family always tended to put off until the last minute. Evan and Mya would then be attending pre-school year teacher conference days at their respective schools, followed by opening day of the new school year.

At this point, the junior division competition was finished, and over at the beach, Evan could see Izzy walking into the water in her orange bathing suit for the girls small-fry race. Although Evan was quite sure she could swim the 50-foot distance with no problem, his daughter looked a little bit unsure of herself as she lined up with the other girls to start the race. Evan smiled. Izzy would do just fine. Afterall, a lost penny had turned up on the cabin floor that morning. After the race, the kids would change into dry clothes, and Evan would take the family to Andy's Drive-in to celebrate. The family would then return to their home, Buker Cottage. Izzy would probably want to take out her paddleboard, and Jeffery would most likely want to take out the motorboat and go fishing. Mya would no doubt tell both of them to stay within the cove and would insist that Izzy wear a life jacket. They would most likely protest. After all, there was a loon nest in the far corner of the cove that Jeff would have to avoid, and of course, he would have to stay clear of Koasek Beach. That would make finding a good fishing spot difficult, and no doubt his sister would attempt to guide her paddleboard toward his spot, just to annoy him. It would be just one more of those priceless memories that could only happen because the children were now being raised on the lake at Buker Cottage, exactly as Evan and Mya had hoped. Later, after the kids returned to shore, the sun would be setting, and the breeze would die down leaving the water smooth, with hardly a ripple. That's when Evan and Mya would uphold their own evening ritual, a canoe ride across the mirror-like surface of Evergreen Lake. Literally, living their dream.

(End)

Transitions of a Band Director

Chapter 1
The Festival Trip

The sound of the rain drops on the skylights were all Eric could hear as he switched on the lights to the music room. A tropical type of rain shower such as this wasn't common in Maine this time of year. They were more likely to occur in the late summer.

"Good thing we're not doing a marching rehearsal outside today," Eric thought to himself as he opened the door to his office.

In another week and a half, his band would be marching in the local Memorial Day parade. However, today was trip day, the annual field trip by the music department of Bayside High School. During each of his twelve years at Bayside, Eric would start planning in October for the annual music trip in May. Some years, he would take his students to see a Broadway musical in New York City or Boston. Other Years, he would take them to compete in a music festival. This year was a festival year, and Eric would be taking his students to the Metropolitan Music Festival, an event held in conjunction with the Six Flags Great Adventure Amusement Park in New Jersey. The festival format was simple. In the morning, Eric's Band, Choir, Select Choir and Jazz Band would perform before a panel of judges. The students would then spend the afternoon in the amusement park. Around suppertime, there would be an awards ceremony where the results of the competition would be announced, after which, the group would board their buses for the trip back home to Maine. Eric listened to the raindrops on the skylights. The rain seemed to be subsiding. Hopefully by the time the motor coaches arrived the rain will have ended. Eric knew it wouldn't be long until students started arriving with their luggage and that's why he arrived early at school today. He turned on his computer and did a final check of instructions for his sub. If all the music students were going on this trip, there would be no need for a substitute teacher for Eric at all. However, almost a dozen of the music students were staying behind for various reasons.

Eric heard the door to the music room open. In walked Matt, Eric's lead alto saxophone player, with his luggage. "Hi Mr. Matthews," Matt said. "Where do you want me to put my luggage?"

Eric scanned the room for a moment. "How about against the back wall?" he replied.

"Will do," said Matt as he took his suitcase to the back wall. "See you later," he said as he headed out the door.

Eric knew that Matt was a diligent student and was probably going to see all of his teachers before school started to check on his assignments. No sooner did Matt leave, when Paul, the school Principal walked into the room.

"Hi Eric, I saw your car and thought I'd check with you. Is everything all set?"

"If you can make the rain go away, that would be great," replied Eric.

"I'll see what I can do," quipped Paul, "I understand some kids are staying here?"

"A few," replied Eric, "I emailed the list to Veronica. A couple of them have after-school jobs and did not arrange for time off with their bosses. Three athletes, two members of the baseball team and one on the softball team are unwilling to miss their games tomorrow. Jamie Collins said she couldn't go on the trip because she had to babysit her younger brother and sister. Others did not participate in the fundraising events and couldn't raise the money necessary to go on the trip. Unfortunate, they have no idea what they might possibly be missing out on." Motioning to Eric's open briefcase, Paul continued, "Doing final preparations?"

"Just double checking to make sure my music is all in order as well as music for the judges. All of the choral pieces the choirs will be performing appear to be intact, as well as the jazz band pieces. As far as concert band pieces go, the R.B. Hall march, David Schafer's 'Bravada Esprit,' and the Tomasso Albinoni 'Adagio,' I think we're good.

"I really enjoyed the performance of the 'Adagio' at the Spring Concert," said Paul, "I think the kids performed it splendidly. It's a beautiful baroque piece."

"Yes, it is," Agreed Eric, "I discovered it in an unused folder in the band's music library a few months ago. It's arranged for band by a European band arranger, which was unique for American band music, but it's also out of print, which unfortunately is not that unique. When I first started the piece, the students were largely unimpressed at first. After all, it's hard for a three-hundred-year-old piece to hold its own against today's rock music."

"But they did a great job performing it at the concert," said Paul,

"Yes," agreed Eric, "that's why I decided to include the piece in the band's performance at the festival."

Satisfied that everything was in order, Eric placed the music folder in his briefcase.

"Alright," said Paul. "Well, let me know if there's anything you need."

"Will do," replied Eric. "Thanks Paul."

With that, Paul left the music room just as more students came in, dropping off their luggage. By the time that the home room bell rang, the music room was nearly filled with suitcases, overnight bags, and the like. At that point, Chris, the assistant principal, walked into the music room and whistled. Gesturing to the luggage, he said, "Wow! It's a good thing you're not going to try and teach with all this stuff in here."

"Yeah," Eric agreed.

"The coaches have just arrived," Chris added, "they're waiting in the bus circle."

"Great. What time do you expect to have the students called down here?"

"About ten minutes into 1st period," answered Chris.

"That sounds good," replied Eric. "Any chance we can have them called to the auditorium, so we don't have to go through the pre-trip logistics in here?" Chris thought for a moment. "I don't think there are any classes scheduled for the auditorium during 1st period, but I'll check."

"That would be great," replied Eric. "Thanks."

About 15 minutes into the 1st period class, Eric could hear the voice of Mrs. Whitney, one of the office secretaries over the intercom.

"Sorry for the interruption," she said, "but at this time, the students going on the music field trip please report to the auditorium."

Eric checked with his sub one last time, then grabbed his briefcase and headed for the auditorium. Alan was waiting for him when he arrived. Alan, the school's Health teacher, was one of three staff members that Eric and Chris recruited as chaperones for the trip. The others, Mrs. Brown, an English teacher, and Miss Gardiner, a Special Ed. teacher's assistant were coming in with the students.

"Hey," Alan said, "it looks like the rain has stopped, and the sun is trying to come out. It looks like we'll be able to do the luggage check outside after all."

Eric nodded as he sat behind a small table on the stage. He opened his briefcase and took out his notes for this meeting, as well as four stacks of papers to be distributed to the students and chaperones: 1) copies of the trip itinerary; 2) the hotel room assignment sheets; 3) sheets listing the groups of students assigned to each chaperone; and 4) Bus assignments. Once everyone was seated, Eric began the pre-trip meeting by taking attendance, and then introducing the parent chaperones, so the students could identify who their chaperones were. He then elaborated on some of the finer points of the itinerary. He reminded the students about the luggage checks that he had talked to them about the previous day, and how that procedure will occur. Finally, he reiterated the behavior guidelines that he had also gone over the previous day in class. He gave them a final warning that any flagrant violation of the behavior guidelines would mean no more music field trips. With that, he asked Chris and the other chaperones if they had anything to add. No one spoke up, and Eric told everyone to get their luggage and proceed to their bus for the luggage check. Some of the students cheered as they headed out the auditorium doors. Eric went back to the music room to get his own overnight bag and headed for the buses. As he walked out the front door of the school, he observed that the luggage checks had already started. In front of one bus, Chris and Alan were checking the boys' luggage, while in front of the other bus Mrs. Brown and Miss Gardiner were checking the girls'. Once everything was loaded onto the buses, and everyone had gotten into their seats, Eric asked the chaperones on each bus to take a final attendance. Once the chaperones confirmed that everyone was where they were supposed to be, Eric called the school's main office on his cell phone and told them that attendance was confirmed, and the buses were leaving. He then nodded to the bus driver, and thus began the field trip, one that Eric would forever remember.

Chapter 2
The Festival Trip, Continued

It was just before 6 pm that the buses pulled into the hotel outside of Trenton, where the group was to stay. Eric used the bus intercom to remind the students that they had fifteen minutes to bring their luggage to their rooms, inspect their room and report any damage to their chaperone, and be back on the bus to go to the local shopping mall. Not wanting to lose any of their shopping time in the mall, the students were very efficient in carrying out their instructions. The buses then proceeded to the mall. The students knew that they had ninety minutes to have supper in the food court and spend the rest of the time shopping. At the end of the ninety-minute mall time everyone was back on the bus with the exception of a couple of students. When the errant students arrived at the bus they were berated by their peers. After all, the tardiness of these students was cutting into everyone's pool time back at the hotel. Eric had reserved the pool for a two-hour slot, and now the students were upset because they were running behind schedule. When they arrived back at the hotel, most of the students changed into their bathing suits at what seemed lightning speed. When pool time ended, the students returned to their rooms for room check and to get ready for bed. Chris led the chaperones going from room to room making sure all the students were in their proper rooms, and everyone settled in for the night.

In the morning, Eric was dressing when he heard a knock on his door, it was Chris. "Just checking in," he said, "getting everyone up on time was a challenge, but the chaperones were up to the task, and everyone is heading for breakfast now."

"Sounds good," replied Eric.

The group arrived at the first judging venue pretty much on time. The choral groups performed first, in a local church. Eric did not care for the acoustics of the room, and the piano was old, and not in the best of shape. However, the students performed well, and he didn't think he could have expected more from them. Satisfied with their performance, the group then proceeded to a high school next door to the church where the band and jazz band would perform. Each group is given a limited amount of warm-up time in a side room prior to performing. During Bayside's warm-up time things were a bit chaotic, with students getting organized, and ready to perform. For some reason, tuning the kids was difficult that morning, and in the end, the band didn't really get to warm-up very much. When they were called to the stage, there was more chaos, as everyone scrambled to make sure they brought everything they needed to the stage. The jazz band performed first, followed by the concert band.

For the groups' introductions, the announcer had a very professional sounding voice as he said, "OUR NEXT PERFORMING GROUP, FROM BAYSIDE, MAINE, IS THE BAYSIDE REGIONAL HIGH SCHOOL CONCERT BAND UNDER THE DIRECTION OF ERIC MATTHEWS. THEY WILL PERFORM THE 'FORT POPHAM MARCH' BY R.B. HALL, 'ADAGIO' BY TOMASSO ALBINONI, AND 'BRAVADA ESPRIT' BY DAVID SHAFFER."

The first piece each group performs is considered a warm-up piece, and as such, is not judged. For Eric, the R.B. Hall march was a natural choice. R.B. Hall was a cornet soloist and band director from Maine, a preeminent composer of marches in the late 1800's. In fact, when John Phillip Sousa took his band to tour Europe, he included several R.B. Hall marches in his repertoire. Eric knew that the kids sounded good on the piece, and even though the piece wasn't being judged, the judges would be listening to how well the group played. The next piece was the Albinoni "Adagio," and right from the opening notes Eric realized that this was not going to be a typical performance. One always has to expect that in most performances involving high school students, there are going to be some glitches and unplanned errors, but on this day, with this piece, at this venue, there were no glitches, no errors, no unexpected difficulties. The band sounded well balanced, with excellent intonation, and the kids played with emotion, and superior musicality. As the piece progressed, their emotion intensified. By the time they got to the end of the piece, Eric almost stopped conducting. He was feeling overwhelmed.

For so many years as a band director, Eric lived for exactly this type of performance from his students and to his surprise, he started crying, right in front of the band, in front of the judges, and in front of the audience. The music being produced by his students was so beautiful, he couldn't help it. He somehow was able to hold it together to the end of the piece, and then he completely broke down. He couldn't even turn around to acknowledge the applause from the audience. As quick as he could, Eric scrambled to pull himself together, as the group still had the David Shaffer piece to perform.

When they finished their performance and left the stage, some band members from the school that they were performing in, who were there to help with the festival, rushed up to the Bayside kids, congratulating them on their performance. Eric was very proud of his students and told them so as they loaded their equipment onto the buses. As the afternoon progressed in the amusement park, all Eric could think about was the upcoming awards ceremony, and reading what the judges had to say about their performance.

In the late afternoon, all of the students and staff from all of the participating schools in the festival gathered in the Six Flags picnic grove for the awards ceremony. At first, all the directors were called up to the front, partially to receive applause from the students but also to receive directors' gifts from the festival and to receive their score sheets. As soon as Eric sat down, he opened up the folder to look at Bayside's score sheets. On the left side of the score sheet were the judge's comments. He scanned down the sheet, and saw a parade of glowing comments, all positive, and no negative comments. What the heck! Eric thought to himself. After all, how can one expect to improve on their performance if the judges don't provide any constructive comments on the sheet.

He then looked over on the right side of sheet, which contained the caption scores. Then his eye caught the total score at the bottom of the sheet, a score of 100 points out of a possible 100, a perfect score. Again, tears started welling up in his eyes. Eric could probably count on one hand the directors he knew of whose groups received perfect scores. He waited until the awards ceremony ended, and then called the band over to where he was sitting.

"This is the second time you all have made me cry today," he said to them as he showed them the score sheet.

The reaction from the students was almost one of disbelief.

"Wow!" exclaimed Matt as he and the other students examined the scoresheet. "We did this?"

"You certainly did," replied Eric, "and I'm very proud of you."

As Eric was putting the scoresheets in his briefcase, his thoughts harkened back to his younger days at the Maine All-State Festival. Through most of Eric's career, he was the sole music teacher in whatever school he taught in. As such, one of his duties as the sole music teacher was to chaperone students from his school attending music festivals. So, when one of his students was accepted to the Maine All-State band, Eric also attended the All-State festival as the student's chaperone. The state music teachers association also offered a conference for music teachers running concurrently with the festival. And although Eric got a lot out of some of the conference sessions, he also enjoyed viewing the All-State band in rehearsal for the All-State concert. Now it almost goes without saying that the All-State band consists of the very best high school musicians that the state has to offer. Entering the rehearsal room and seeing the full group there is daunting enough. Eric had to wonder how many future music educators, and perhaps even future professional musicians or professional music professors were sitting in this group. However, that wasn't all. It was also common for the All-State committee to bring in a nationally known conductor to direct the group. In this case, the conductor of the band was the great Warner Tratelli of Manchester State University. Mr. Tratelli had a way of bringing out the very best musicality of the kids. In a lot of ways, he personified the type of conductor that inspired countless music students to become music educators. As Eric listened to the rehearsal, the band played through a very lyrical passage of the music and did a very nice job of it. Tratelli stopped the group to compliment them on how well they did. As he talked to them, Eric could see tears streaming down his cheeks. There was nothing phony about it. He was really moved by how the kids played, and he finally had to take out a handkerchief to wipe away the tears. As for the kids, the idea that they could play well enough to induce this kind of reaction from their conductor was eminently satisfying.

Until today, Eric had never cried in front of his students, but on this particular day, as he was making his way from the picnic grove back to the buses in the parking lot, Eric couldn't help but wonder if over the years, he had become the next Warner Tratelli.

Chapter 3
The Nightmare Begins

It would have been nice if Eric could say that his subsequent years at Bayside were just as successful. Unfortunately, that was not to be the case. Certainly, the year started out fairly successfully. The band did wonderfully well performing at the usual events during the fall and the winter. But during Christmas vacation Eric started hearing on the news about this newly discovered virus in Asia that was very contagious and was expected to spread to the United States. In March, COVID-19 hit Maine, and the effects were severe. Like all other schools, Bayside went into immediate shutdown. During the first week of the shutdown, Eric attended emergency faculty meetings at the school to set up and plan for remote learning.

"I understand this is daunting," Paul said as he addressed the faculty, "but everyone is going to need to learn how to use Zoom, how to produce instruction videos, how to transcribe lesson and exercise sheets into PDF's, and how to fashion lessons that can be conducted over the internet. We will work on most of this in faculty meetings, but right now, my question is how many of you think you may need extra technology coaching?"

As one who was not particularly savvy in technology, Eric raised his hand, along with several other teachers.

"Okay," said Paul, "Those of you raising your hands coordinate with Chris to schedule individual coaching sessions. Everyone else, you can spend the time preparing on your own."

The following week, chaos ensued as the school struggled to find out which students had computers at home that would allow them to access instruction, and which students needed to sign out school laptops. For families that did not have internet, every effort was made to get them connected, but some families still fell through the cracks.

Like the teachers, the majority of the students tried to make the best of this difficult situation, but unfortunately, a portion of the students regarded this interruption as an unexpected vacation. It took Eric weeks to fully establish communication with all his students, and even then, a handful of them never responded. There was a member of Eric's choir, a senior, who was an excellent singer, but she was one of those students that did well in music, but not so well in the rest of her subjects. Eric worried that she was showing signs of dropping out of school. Both he and Chris talked to the student, pointing out that so long as she stayed in school, she could continue to sing in the choir hoping that would motivate her. Eric decided not tell her that he had also ordered an award for her. He planned to award her with the outstanding vocalist award at graduation. Unfortunately, now that COVID had hit, he lost all contact with her. She didn't respond to any of his emails, nor did she respond to any phone calls from the school. She never did graduate, and Eric was never able to present the award to her.

Using Zoom for band instruction was really difficult. It would have been great if Eric could just say, "OK everyone, take out the first song and we'll play it together. Ready? One, Two, Three, Go!" and everyone would play the piece together. Unfortunately, that just doesn't work. First of all, Zoom has a sound delay integrated into its software. This causes multiple delays of various lengths when an entire group starts playing or singing at once. In addition, the oscillators of the computer that reproduce sounds have only so much capacity. When the entire band plays, the oscillators become overloaded, and the computer decides which incoming signals it will produce, and which ones it will ignore.

But the one thing that Eric was having a really hard time with was student irresponsibility. One day, he was listening to students playing an exercise sheet that he had designed. It would have been great if he could listen to the entire band play the exercise sheet at once, but because of the limitations of Zoom, he had to listen to the students individually.

"Okay," he said, "Jimmy, let me hear you play the fourth line of the exercise sheet."

After a long pause, Jimmy said, "Uuunn, I don't have my trumpet with me. It's in school."

Eric was upset. "Jimmy, do you realize the problems that your neglect is now going to cause me?"

Jimmy looked away from the camera with a guilty look on his face.

Eric continued, "Now, I'm going to have to go looking to find your trumpet, label it, and place it in the lobby of the main entrance of the school. Then I have to inform the secretaries in the main office. That means that your irresponsibility will be causing them extra work."

"Sorry," Jimmy replied.

Eric continued, "When your mom comes to the school to pick up your trumpet, she will have to come to the main entrance and ring the doorbell. She won't be allowed into the building because all the doors will be locked. She'll have to identify herself over the intercom to the office secretary, and the secretary will have to look through the lobby among the books, papers, file folders, and other materials left in the lobby by the faculty for dozens of students to pick up. Once she locates the trumpet, she will have to bring it over to the main door to give it to your mother." Eric stopped talking. It was obvious that Jimmy was tuning him out. "You do want to pass this class, don't you?"

"Yes," said Jimmy.

"Well then, I would strongly suggest you be more responsible from this point forward."

Chapter 4
The Virtual Project

As April began, Eric realized that he needed to come up with a plan to keep his students active in music. There was no state festival to take the students to. There would also be no Spring Concert, and no Spring Trip. There would be no Memorial Day Parade, and for graduation, it was decided that for safety reasons, the band would not participate. What kind of alternative could he possibly come up with? Eric spent a lot of time on the internet looking for ideas. One of the interesting developments on the internet during COVID was a dramatic increase in virtual performances. All the members of an ensemble would record themselves, and the recordings would be mixed together. Visually, the screen would show multiple windows, one for each participant.

"Could this work?" Eric asked himself. He knew he didn't have the sophisticated digital equipment that the producers of some of these professional looking virtual recordings must have been using. "I wonder if I can cobble something together that would work with the resources I have," he thought. Eric decided to give it a shot.

The next day, he announced to his band and choir over Zoom, "We're going to try an experiment."

After explaining to his students what virtual performance was, he encouraged the students to check out YouTube to view examples of it. He then told the students, "We're going to divide the band into small ensembles, duets, trios, quartets. If there's someone you wish to be in an ensemble with, let me know. I'm going to choose pieces for each ensemble to play. Choir people, you will all perform the same song. I'll let you know which one when I decide. I'm going to make a recording of your part for each of you. I will email them to you, and I want you to practice with the recording. We won't be posting anything to YouTube, but I would like to post them on the school web site."

The reaction from the students was mixed. Some of them were excited about this new project, while others, not so much. Some of them were having a hard time conceptualizing what Eric was asking of them, and he had to go over the explanation multiple times. In the next few days, Eric sent out recordings of his assignment to the students. Now came the challenging part, explaining the procedure to the students.

"You will need two digital devices to make this work," he said. "For many of you, your cell phone may work as one of the devices. I know that many of you have used your cell phones to record worksheets. You will also need a set of earbuds or headphones. If you can't use your cell phone to record yourself, then you will need two computers."

"If anyone needs to borrow my cell phone, we can probably figure something out," said Elizabeth, one of the more social students in the band.

"I'm sure that will be helpful," said Eric, "but you all need to know that I am considering this to be the major project of the semester. In fact, you should consider this your final exam."

Eric could hear groans from some of the students. "I need you all to take this assignment seriously, and I'm giving fair warning that if anyone blows off this assignment, I will not be sympathetic when it comes to end of the year grades." Eric listened for reaction.

There was silence.

"Alright," he said. "For those of you that need to locate the devices you need, or go out and get some ear buds, I'll give you a couple of days. In the meantime, keep practicing with the recordings I sent you, and be ready to follow my instructions after the weekend."

The following Monday, Eric picked up where he left off. The first thing he asked was, "I want to know if everyone checked their computers and cellphones over the weekend. Is everyone prepared to do their recordings this week?"

A few students spoke up.

"I have to use my sister's cell phone," Hannah said.

"I've got it worked out that I can do it with my laptop, and my father's computer," said Walter.

"I think I'm in trouble," Jessica chimed in. "Our internet is so unreliable that when I record myself, the size of the file is too big to send to you."

"Alright," replied Eric. "How many of you are having difficulties similar to Jessica?"

Six students raised their hands.

"Okay," said Eric. "After we're done with class today, I want you six to stay online with me, and I'll try to help each of you troubleshoot your situation."

"What does that mean?" asked Faith, a special ed. student who loved being in band.

"That means he'll try and help you fix it," said Jeff, a somewhat hyper drummer.

"We'll talk about these things later," said Eric. "Right now, I want those of you with working equipment to pay close attention while I give you instructions. I'll send these out in an email later, but if you're confused by any of the directions I give, tell me."

Eric paused to make sure he had everyone's attention. "Those of you recording on your cell phone should first plug your earphones or earbuds into your computer and pull up the practice recording I sent you, that you should have been working on. Next, put your cell phone on 'record' and place it where it will capture you playing. Once your cell phone is recording, start the practice recording of the piece on your computer. As you listen through your ear buds to the practice recording, try to play along with the piece as exactly as you can. Do at least three takes and send me the best one."

After a couple of days, Eric started receiving recordings from the students. Now, his work was just beginning. Even though they were playing along with a recording, many students committed several timing errors. Eric had to use the editing features of the Audacity audio program that he had downloaded to cut out fractions of a second on some of the students' parts so the recordings would stay in sync. It took hours and hours to edit all of the student recordings. He then had to download the student recordings into a video editing program, along with the master audio recording. This also took a huge amount of time, and by the time school ended in June, Eric only had one video ready to be posted on the school web site. It took until mid-summer to prepare the rest of the videos. Some of them turned out nice, others, not so much. Unfortunately, some of the students did not do the project. Eric gave them a grade of 'F' which lowered their grade in Band considerably. And yet, there were a few students that did not submit any recordings of themselves at all over the entire three months, no exercises, Etudes, worksheets, nothing. Those students Eric flunked for the Fourth quarter grading period. He hated doing it. In all the years he taught, he had never flunked so many students at one time. But what else could he do? These students didn't show any evidence that they were improving their playing skills or their musicianship. In fact, Eric didn't have any evidence that they were practicing at all. He gave a heads-up to Paul and Chris when he submitted his grades. The fall-out from flunking so many students was that most of them dropped Band the following year.

Chapter 5
COVID, the Second Year

The first few months of COVID were in some ways traumatizing. As the school year came to an end, the faculty at Bayside High School spent a lot of time in meetings discussing the three-month shutdown, and the effects of remote learning. Eric remembered at one point reading a post from some people down south, maybe Florida or Alabama, saying, "Hey! This remote learning stuff is pretty cool. We should consider doing it permanently."

All Eric could think of was, "What Idiots!"

One of the things the faculty at Bayside learned early on was that remote learning was a poor substitute for learning in the classroom. It was clear that they had to find some way to bring students back into the building, and as Music Teacher, it was up to Eric to find a way to make his classes work. He did a lot of searching on the internet trying to find the most recent research on COVID. He came across a study done at the University of Colorado which focused on aerosol production playing wind instruments. He studied the data carefully, how far aerosols could be propelled, which instruments were more problematic than others, and what possible modifications could be implemented. When the Principal announced that the school was going to receive funds for COVID, Eric was ready. He went to see Paul, the Principal.

He knocked on the open door and said, "Hi Paul, I have a plan. Here are some funding requests for necessary materials and equipment."

Paul looked at the funding requests. "I don't think we'll have a problem with any of this," he said. "But I think we should discuss where you will be teaching. I'd like to move your classes into the auditorium."

"The auditorium," Eric said thoughtfully. "Yeah, I can do that. I just hadn't considered it."

"I think it would be for the best," Paul replied. "You could teach from the stage, and we can spread the students across the seating area."

"Those auditorium chairs don't provide the best support for playing instruments," Eric pointed out. "Utilize chairs from your music room as you see fit, just remember, the students will need to wipe them down at the end of each class."

"Along with wiping down their music stand and shield," Eric added.

Paul looked confused. "Their what?"

"Plexiglass shields," Eric explained. "They take a music stand base, but instead of putting a music stand top on it. They put a 2 1/2 by 3-foot piece of plexiglass instead. When the student sits down to play, they put their music stand in front of them, and behind the music stand the place their shield to help catch aerosols."

"Really, that's interesting," Paul replied.

"You'll find them on the equipment funding list I gave you," Eric added.

Paul looked at the list, and then said, "Excellent, draw up the purchase order requests and send them to Ann ASAP so she can order them now. Hopefully, we'll get them before school opens in September."

"No problem," replied Eric. "Thanks, are there any other issues I should know about?"

Paul checked his computer, and said, "Yes, we are changing our class schedule to a 4 by 4 block schedule."

"Why?" interrupted Eric. "I hate that schedule."

"The overall goal is to minimize the amount person-to person contact in the building," explained Paul. "That is the school board's directive. The school day will be divided into four 90-minute classes. Students will attend those four classes for the entire semester and will receive a full credit for each class when the semester ends at mid-year. They will then attend four different classes the next semester."

"I've taught long enough to know that a 4x4 schedule has very negative effects on a music program, and it's well documented," said Eric.

"That would be unfortunate," replied Paul, "but it's not the only change. The superintendent and school board have designated that there will be a two-day rotation where only half the students can be in the building at one time. This means that every other day, only the students whose last names begin with A-L will be allowed to attend school in person. The remaining students will view class remotely over Zoom. The following day, the roles will reverse with the M-Z students attending in person. With only four class periods in a school day, that means that each teacher will teach only three classes. The remaining period for teachers will be a prep period, and with these changes, I'm sure you realize that teachers will need all the preparation they can get. Your class schedule will consist of two band classes, one in the morning and one in the afternoon with different students, and a choir class."

"Oh hell," said Eric, "Are you sure we'll be able to function this way?"

"I don't know," replied Paul, "I only know that we have to try."

"Any other wonderful news you need to lay on me?"

Paul smiled. "I think that will be sufficient for now. Keep me informed on your progress."

"Will do," said Eric as he got up to leave.

Two weeks before school was scheduled to start, Eric emailed music students and their parents, telling them that he was scheduling a Zoom meeting about a week before the school year was to begin. During the evening meeting, his email said, he would explain all the modifications and protocols necessary for band and chorus classes the coming school year. The next week, on the evening of the meeting, Eric had about two dozen students and parents attend virtually. He began the meeting by explaining the new scheduling changes and how the class schedule was going to work. He then explained the class format changes and explained the rules that needed to be followed in class in terms of class set-up and protocols. Fortunately, the new plexiglass shields that Eric had ordered arrived a couple of days before the meeting, and he was able to show them to everyone over Zoom.

"Something else," Eric added. "Brass players, that is to say trumpet, trombone, euphonium, tuba, and french horn players will need to use bell coverings on their instruments. Mrs. Erskine, our Home Ec./Life Skills teacher is going to make them for us."

Eric approached Mrs. Erskine because he felt that the brass instrument bell coverings offered by retailers were very expensive. After an explanation of what bell coverings were, and how they would be utilized, Mrs. Erskine agreed to make them for free. Touched by her generosity, Eric sent a substantial donation to her after-school club.

"Mr. Matthews," said one of the parents, "what about the woodwind instruments?"

"Good question," replied Eric. "According to the data I've seen, the aerosol production of the woodwind instruments does not rise to the same threat level as brass instruments, except for the flute. Covering the flute isn't going to work, but I think by separating the players and using the shields, we should be in good shape."

Eric paused for a moment. "Alright, last issue," he told the students and parents online, "I will end each class 10 minutes early, so that you can put away your instruments, grab a spray bottle of antiseptic, and wipe down your music stands and shields. Percussionists will need to wipe down their equipment, as well as any school-owned drumsticks and mallets. Are there any questions about this or any other issue?"

Hearing nothing, Eric said, "Well then, that should do it. Thank you everyone for tuning in tonight, and good luck to us all."

On the first day of class, Eric reviewed all the class procedures for students that did not attend the Zoom meeting and passed out music. The second day, they began playing and Eric's disappointment was obvious. Only a few students were able to navigate the music he passed out, and as far as he could tell, the rest of the students did not practice at all during the summer. The next day, with a different set of students, the same result. The major factor that Eric found very difficult was that the administration insisted that the teachers split their class time between the students that were there live, and the students that were attending class virtually. It was very difficult, and to top it off, there was one student in choir that refused to attend school in person at all. Moreover, she had no intention of attending any performances. Eric was very upset about this. The music classes are participatory in nature, and non-participating students are antithetical to the goals of the class. He brought this situation to the attention of the administration, with the hope that she could be removed from his class and given another class to study instead. Eric was told by the administration that she had the right not to participate in person, and that he would have to live with the situation. What a disappointment, the first of many that the new school year would bring.

Chapter 6
Time for a Concert

As expected, the switch to the 4x4 block schedule took its toll on the music enrollment. The membership in both band and chorus dropped by 50% from the previous year. Despite a very slow start to the school year, the students eventually showed a considerable amount of progress. At the start of November, Eric sent a memo to Paul requesting to hold a Winter Concert in December. Eric knew the request would be forwarded to the superintendent, and that the school board might also be involved in the decision. He outlined the steps he would be willing to take in order to hold the event. The Bayside High School sports teams were active, but followed the rule that for games, only family members of the students involved were allowed as spectators. Eric indicated that he would follow this same policy for the concert. He also said that he would establish a 30-foot buffer zone from the stage to the first row of audience members. Band members would remain masked, until it was time to perform, and the set-up on stage would include the plexiglass shields which would affect the sound of the band, but it couldn't be helped. In addition, the concert would be spread over two nights, with the chorus performing the first night, and the band performing the next. This would also allow each concert to be fairly short, less than an hour.

A few days later, Paul called Eric into his office.

"Alright Eric," Paul told him. "Your plan for the concert has been approved."

"That's Great," Eric replied.

"Well," continued Paul, "the school board has set some additional requirements."

"What kind of requirements?" asked Eric.

"You will need to issue tickets numbered to correspond to the available seats in the auditorium. Tickets need to be limited to three tickets per student, and although family members will be allowed to sit together, family groups would have to be distanced. Masking will be mandated for everyone. I'll have Ruth provide you with seating charts for the auditorium, one for the first night, and one for the second. Chris has agreed to screen the audience at the door."

"It sounds like I need to recruit students to act as ushers," added Eric.

"I was about to suggest that," said Paul. "Also, you have a tradition of holding a reception in the cafeteria for students and their parents after concerts, correct?"

"That's correct," replied Eric, "I'm guessing that's a tradition we're going to have to scrap?"

"Yes, we don't want anyone hanging around after the concert. We want parents and students out of the building as soon as the concert is over."

"Alright," said Eric. "It's going to be one strange concert, but at least the kids will get a chance to perform."

"I understand, but at this point it's the best we can do," replied Paul.

About two weeks prior to the concert, Eric took some time out of class to call the students, one by one, up to his podium on stage, seniors first, followed by juniors, sophomores, and finally freshmen. He allowed each student to choose where in the auditorium their family members should sit, taking care that each family group was properly distanced. In the following days, He sorted the numbered tickets into three-ticket packets for each family and distributed the packets to the students.

On the nights of the concerts, the students performed well. A reporter from the local weekly newspaper came and took photos that were published in the following week's edition. Apparently, it was big news for a school to be holding a concert, while the music programs at most of the area schools were pretty much inactive. In fact, there were some schools that refused to allow their band students to play any wind instruments, and the band directors were forced to conduct classes with everyone playing percussion instruments.

As the first half of the year drew to a close, Eric was feeling exceedingly frustrated by the limitations in his job brought on by the pandemic. He was determined to make a go of it, but he constantly worried about his ability to provide quality instruction to students given all these limitations. Still, every now and then, he would notice an individual student making a major stride. Maybe it would be an increase in their music reading skills, or an improvement in their technique. It was heartening enough to motivate him to push on. For the time being anyway.

Chapter 7
Is it Time?

As the second half of the school year started in January, Eric was feeling tired. In fact, there were days when he was feeling downright fatigued. Some days were worse than others.

"I don't like your color. You don't look well," his wife, Lorina, kept telling him. "And it looks like you're losing weight."

One day, Eric was having a particularly difficult time. He thought to himself, "Maybe it's time to take stock of the situation. Maybe it's time to think about retirement."

The very idea that he would think about retiring shocked him. It was something he had never considered before. Eric loved teaching. He always felt that he would teach until he couldn't physically do it anymore. He would even joke with Paul about being wheeled into the music room in his hospital bed to teach. But teaching during COVID was very trying. Even though Eric felt he was doing as well as he possibly could, he still had the nagging suspicion that it just wasn't enough.

Eric thought to himself, "I'm 68 years old. I have limited mobility and have to walk with a cane. I can't even stand to conduct my groups. I have to conduct sitting on a stool."

A couple of days later, Chris took him aside and said, "Did you realize that when I came into the teachers' room this morning that you were fast asleep in your chair?"

Eric was stunned. Was it possible that it was time to pack it in and he hadn't realized it?

Eric started giving it a lot of thought, and a few days later, he had the chance to speak with Paul in private. "I wanted to give you a heads-up," he told Paul. "I'm considering retiring at the end of the school year."

"I'm very sorry to hear that," said Paul. "Let me know what you decide."

"You may be waiting right up till the May 1st deadline."

"That's fine," replied Paul. "Take all the time you need."

Every day, Eric would think about it, stay, or go, teach or retire, pros and cons. No doubt about it, this was going to be a very difficult decision.

In the meantime, there was the rest of the school year to plan and think about. The state music teachers association decided that it would hold its annual Solo & Ensemble festival, but remotely. Normally, students would prepare solos or ensembles, duets, trios, quartets, etc. and perform their pieces in front of judges for a rating. However, this year, the decision was made that the directors would submit videos of their students performing their pieces. The judges would evaluate the performances virtually. Eric submitted four videos of students performing solos. All four received superior or excellent ratings from the judges. Eric's thoughts harkened back to a time many years ago, when he would take two busloads of students to a Solo & Ensemble Festival. How things had changed.

One day, Eric went to Paul's office. "I know this is pushing the envelope," he told Paul. "But I would like to plan a festival trip."

At first, Paul was silent. "Do you really think you can pull this off?" he asked.

"I don't know," replied Eric, "but I'd like to try. Nothing fancy like New Jersey, but maybe something close like Massachusetts or New Hampshire."

"Well," said Paul, "at this point, some of the COVID restrictions are being lifted as more research is being done on the virus. I'm thinking it's possible, but it may be very difficult to navigate. I'm sure the school board would hold off on approving the trip until their May meeting."

Eric thought for a moment and said, "When I talk to the bus company, hotel and festival people, I'll make sure that they all agree that in the event that the school board doesn't approve the trip, we'll receive a refund."

"A good idea," agreed Paul. "Check for the COVID protocols at all of the venues."

"Will do," Eric replied.

When Eric announced his plans to the students, the upperclassmen, the ones that had travelled to the New Jersey festival, were very excited. The freshmen and sophomores seemed unsure. Eric started his trip planning, which consisted of several phone calls. Normally, to book a motorcoach in February for a May trip was usually next to impossible. But with COVID, not a whole lot of people were travelling, so there were plenty of buses available. The same thing with the hotel. Availability of rooms was not a problem. He also checked the Six Flags New England web site for their COVID protocols, since that was the amusement park working in conjunction with the festival he was considering.

Once he calculated the per/student cost for their spot on the trip. Eric sent an email to parents outlining plans for the trip and setting up a schedule for those parents that wanted to break up the per/student cost in payments. March 1st arrived, and Eric received initial payments from about a third of the students. This wasn't unusual, and he didn't think much about it. For most students, the financial matters usually worked out. April 1st arrived, and Eric only had payments from half the students. Now, it was time to start checking with individual students. Some of the underclassmen told him that they did not want to go on the trip, while others said that their parents would not allow them to go. In looking at the situation, Eric had to admit that this wasn't going to work. He had done trips in the past where some students stayed home. He was always able to work around the situation and make adjustments in the music so that the students would have a positive musical experience. Eric did precisely that for the group's New Jersey trip two years ago. But this time, he had to admit, he couldn't do this trip with only half a band.

Eric ended up having to cancel the trip. Yes, a number of students were very disappointed, but to say that Eric himself was also disappointed would have been an understatement. It was embarrassing to go to Paul and inform him that the trip was off.

"In all my 46 years as a music educator, I never had to cancel a trip because not enough students participated," he told Paul.

It was also embarrassing to have to refund payments that had already been made by students. The more he thought about it, the more upset he became. Most upsetting of all was that it appeared that he didn't have the trust of those students and parents who wouldn't commit to this project.

He told Paul, "I took the trip planning very seriously and meticulously went over every detail of the trip to make sure that everyone would be safe. If I had come across any potentially dangerous issue, I would have dropped the project right then and there."

It was maddening, and Eric realized that this was the proverbial straw that broke the camel's back, the deciding factor. As it was, trying to deal with performance planning, music program operations, and teaching under COVID conditions was difficult enough, but dealing with fickle students and parents when it came to music activities was a bridge too far. The following day he submitted his letter of retirement.

Chapter 8
The final Performances

The decision was made, the die was cast. This would be the last year of Eric's 46-year career. He hoped that he might find a part-time position somewhere that would allow him to keep teaching, but for now, Eric would need to turn his attention to the final performances of the year. In May, Eric set up a spring concert. He did it the same way he did the Winter Concert, with all the same COVID protocols, separating family groups, buffer zone in front of the stage, one night for chorus, the other for band, etc.

The first concert night, the chorus performance, went as well as he could have expected, and he was hoping for similar results the following night with the band. The following day, Eric held a dress rehearsal on the stage for the band during the afternoon band class. It worked out well, because all he had to do was tell the students not to put any chairs or equipment away, just their instruments. This would save a considerable amount of time before the concert because the set-up was already in place.

When school was over, Eric went to a faculty committee meeting, and after the meeting, he headed to his office to catch up on a bit of paperwork. As Eric approached the music room, the door was open, but two students blocked his way.

"Sorry Mr. Matthews," one of the students said, "but we can't let you in the room."

"Yeah," said the other student. "It's Top Secret, you need to wait in the teachers' room until the coast is clear."

Looking past them into the room, it appeared that these two students were part of a larger group of students, and they were obviously up to something. Eric decided not to challenge the students and went to the teachers' room to wait. When the students told him it was OK to enter the music room, he walked inside and headed to his office. Eric didn't see anything out of the ordinary, but he noticed that the auditorium was all closed up. After spending some time in his office, he went to dress for the concert, and started pre-concert preparations. The students needed to report to the music room when they arrived for the concert. As they arrived, they took out their instruments and started warming up, followed by tuning, and then lining up to move to the stage.

When everything was all set, Eric told the students, "I want to thank you all for working so hard, and I'm looking forward to a great final concert."

He paused to fight back a tear, and then said, "Ok, let's move."

He sent the students to the stage in single file and followed them backstage. He looked out on to the stage and realized what the students had been up to earlier. The front apron of the stage was lined with all of the trophies from the trophy shelf, from one end of the stage to the other, all 42 of them. Earlier, when Eric walked through the music room after their "Top Secret" session, he did not notice that the trophies were missing. Chris stood at the speaker's podium and welcomed the audience to the concert.

"Good evening, everyone," he said. "Welcome to our annual Spring Concert. In fact, tonight's Spring Concert is very special as I am announcing tonight that our Music Director, Mr. Matthews, will be retiring at the end of the school year, and this will be the final Spring Concert of Mr. Matthews's 46-year career."

A smattering of applause broke out in approval of his comments. Chris continued, "The effect of Mr. Matthews's efforts here at Bayside have been incredibly impressive and the 42 trophies that you see here at the front of the stage are testimony to the achievements of Mr. Matthews's students through the 15 years that he has taught here."

More applause, as Chis spoke, Eric realized that placing the trophies at the front of the stage had been his idea.

"What you don't see," Chris continued, "are the prodigious number of plaques, certificates, citations, and awards that we were unable to include on stage tonight. But needless to say, Mr. Matthews will be missed. So, I'd like to ask you all to please stand and welcome Mr. Matthews to his final concert with us."

Cheers rang out. Well, what would pass for cheers with a COVID size audience. Eric smiled and waved as he walked on to the stage. He bowed to the audience, and then took his seat on the conductor's podium. It certainly was a great way to start a concert.

With the concerts finished, Eric still had one more May performance to plan. The previous year's Memorial Day Parade had been canceled in the midst of the pandemic, but this year, the veterans decided that they wanted to resume the event, and asked Eric if it would be possible to have the band march. Eric told them that he couldn't make any promises, but that he would work on it. In past years, the bands from the high school and the middle school would combine into one large group consisting of more than 80 musicians. However, when the middle school band director emailed Eric saying that COVID had put the band program there in very bad shape, and it would not be possible for the middle school band to participate in the parade, it was very bad news indeed. A major setback, to be sure, but Eric wasn't ready to let it stop him just yet. He took out his old email list of former students that had graduated, and put out an email outlining the situation, and saying that if any of them would be willing to march with the high school band, that he would be most appreciative. Within a few days he received responses from two dozen alumni, which would certainly be enough to allow the high school band to march. Eric then turned his attention to the means by which the band could march. The COVID experts were very adamant about marching bands, highly discouraging the idea. The aerosols exhaled by one band member could easily be inhaled by the band member directly following, thereby spreading the infection. However, in recent months, researchers had made discoveries about the COVID virus regarding the outdoors. They found that the virus had a very hard time surviving outdoors, especially if sunlight was present. In addition, even the slightest breeze would help disperse the aerosols, which would make the spread of infection less likely. Eric considered this new information, and with Paul off at a conference, he went to see Chris.

"I have a plan for the parade," he told Chris.

"I had the feeling you probably would," Chris responded.

"Well," said Eric, "I consider this one to be especially brilliant."

"Do Tell!" Chris replied.

"Well, you know I sent out an email to band alumni asking if they would be willing to participate with the band in the parade. Well, I received replies from two dozen alumni, and that will give us enough musicians to put together a respectable size band."

"That sounds great!" Chris commented.

"Now, for the innovative part," Eric continued. "Instead of standard rows of band members, I want to structure the rows in the shape of a 'V,' with a lead marcher in the middle, flanked by two marchers diagonally behind, and more marchers continuing the diagonal line. The second line following will also form the shape of a 'V' but be spaced eight steps, or 15 feet behind, and so on for the remaining lines except for the drummers, who would be in the back and masked. I call it a 'Flying V Formation.' The band will be small enough so that tempo clashes from front to back can be avoided, and each row of players can be safely distanced."

"That is innovative," Chris responded, "I would say go for it."

Eric called the parade chairman and told him that the band would be able to march on Memorial Day, but not in the way they normally did as he explained the situation to them.

About a week before the parade, Eric had the high school band practice the formation, and within a few minutes, it was working perfectly. He even called a reporter at the local weekly newspaper and told him about what he was planning. After all, this wasn't just a good idea, it was innovative, and the Bayside High School Band would probably be the only band in the state marching that day.

Unfortunately, Eric's innovative plan didn't work out. Scattered thunderstorms that morning forced the parade's cancellation. Instead of the parade, there was a ceremony at the middle school. The band performed, but with only half the alumni that Eric was expecting. The veterans were still thankful that the band performed, but Eric's disappointment was obvious.

Chapter 9
The Quick End

Eric would forever remember the day, Wednesday, June 4. It started out like any June day, sunny, with a few clouds, and Eric arrived at school in the morning as he normally did. His lesson plan was fairly straight forward, polishing the band and choir music for graduation, which would be held in a week and a half. He woke up that morning with a pain in his lower backside.

"Must have pulled a muscle," he thought to himself. "It should fade away as the day goes on."

Unfortunately, the pain intensified through the morning, and at lunch time, the school nurse examined Eric.

"This isn't a pulled muscle," she said as she felt around the area. "This is kidney pain!"

Paul immediately sent him home, and he left the school. Eric went home and laid down, hoping the pain would go away. It didn't and he finally decided to go to the emergency room. Maybe it's a kidney stone, he thought to himself. Eric had never experienced a kidney stone, but it seemed to be as logical an explanation as anything else. He walked into the emergency room at the local hospital and told the nurse that he thought he might have a kidney stone. After taking his information, she told him to sit in the waiting room, and after about 30 minutes, Eric was taken into a treatment room. After a short wait, they took him for a CT scan, and brought him back to the treatment room. He waited in the treatment room for a long time, almost two hours. Finally, the emergency room doctor came in to see him.

"Well," the doctor said, "it's not a kidney stone. You have a growth on your kidney."

"A growth?"

"Yes," he said. "Most likely, a tumor."

"Cancerous?" Eric asked.

"Probably, it will require another CT Scan with better contrast to be sure."

"Oh Lord!" Eric exclaimed, staring at the ceiling.

"This may be really serious," the doctor said.

"I'm recommending that we transport you to the hospital in Portland tonight."

"No!" Eric replied. "I don't want to see any doctor in Portland. I want my own doctors around here to take care of this."

They argued back and forth for several minutes. The doctor finally relented, but insisted on several restrictions, complete bedrest until Eric saw his doctors, another CT scan within ten days, no driving, and no work. Eric wasn't even allowed to drive home. He had to call Lorina to come and get him, and their son would need to come and drive Eric's car home. While he was waiting for Lorina and his son to arrive, Eric called Paul to let him know what was going on. At first, Paul was silent, as if he were trying to absorb what Eric was telling him. After all, this meant that Eric would not be able to work with the band and choir on their music for graduation, nor would he even be there for their graduation performances.

"Listen," Paul said, "I want you to concentrate on taking care of yourself. Don't worry about the graduation music, Chris and I will find a way to make it work."

So, to recap, Eric began the day in typical fashion, but by evening, his career was over. There would be no more teaching, no more conducting, no more performances. Eric hadn't even gone home yet, and already he was depressed.

Chapter 11
Dealing With the Medical Profession

To be sure, Eric had a great deal of respect for doctors, nurses, and medical workers, but he believed that the medical profession, in general, badly needed an overhaul. He didn't know if the problem was with overtly oppressive insurance regulations, or overzealous medical executives trying to squeeze efficiencies out of the system. That was not to say that those providing direct care were deficient. Most of the time, he found them to be caring and knowledgeable professionals.

"You know," he told Lorina. "While I'm aware that you've spent your career as a member of the medical profession, I really have to wonder about the profession itself."

"The staff I worked with at the nursing home gave excellent care," Lorina protested. "When the state came in to do inspections, they rarely found a problem."

"I know," replied Eric, "and to be honest, the care I have received as a hospital patient has been excellent. But as an out-patient, perhaps not as much. Many times, it seems that for an out-patient like me, the medical profession operates at two speeds, slow and stop. You know, I believe that if I had taken the emergency room doctor's advice and allowed myself to be transferred to the hospital in Portland, I probably would have received a second CT scan within a couple of days. It's now been three weeks, and they still haven't scheduled the scan for me. Instead, it appears I'm following the out-patient protocol which can best be described as 'Hurry up and Wait.'"

In fact, Eric wasn't able to receive a second CT scan until five weeks after his emergency room diagnosis. Even then, he ended up going to an imaging center down near Portland. His doctors referred him to a local oncologist, but there wasn't much the oncologist could do until Eric's second CT scan took place. He finally met with his oncologist a couple of weeks after the second CT scan, and finally received a formal diagnosis, kidney cancer, Stage 4. His prognosis- less than a year.

When Eric met with his oncologist, he wasn't really sure why he told the doctor that he would be willing to try whatever treatment the doctor would suggest. At this point, Eric was in a very deep depression. He began to think that he had made a dreadful error in deciding to retire. But whatever he ended up believing wouldn't matter because the cancer diagnosis forced the issue. Eric spent most of his days in bed. Back in April, shortly after he sent in his retirement letter, Eric purchased a laptop computer as a retirement gift to himself. The laptop now sat on his chest for most of the day as he lay in bed. He would play games, or cruise the internet, anything to try to distract himself from the situation.

It was now mid-summer, and even though the temperature was approaching 90, Eric felt cold, and constantly wore a sweatshirt. He wasn't interested in eating, though Lorina was usually able to coax him to eat a meal most days, but that was about it. Eric thought it was great of her to leave him alone in bed and let him do his thing, but he soon learned why. While he was spending his day in bed, Lorina was spending her day in the kitchen, crying.

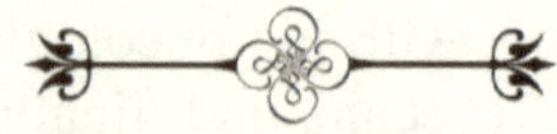

Chapter 12
The Hits Keep On Coming

When Labor Day approached, Eric's depression intensified. He would constantly be looking at the clock, thinking, "If I were in school now, what would I be doing?"

Moreover, the symphony orchestra that Eric had played with for many years had been dormant for the last couple of years due to COVID. It was now starting back up, and Eric wasn't going to be a part of it.

In the meantime, his oncologist came up with a treatment plan for him. Eric would take a daily chemo pill and would go to the infusion clinic once a month for another medication to be given intravenously. The first dose was given to him through the arm, but the oncologist suggested that he have a port inserted just below the skin in his upper chest which would make frequent infusions a lot more tolerable. It was a minor surgical procedure, but soon Eric received a call from the Medication Management division of the hospital, which monitored Eric's Warfarin medication. Eric had been on Warfarin, a blood thinner taken to prevent stroke and the nurse from Medication Management viewed this as a complication.

"We understand that you're scheduled for surgery to insert an infusion port," the nurse said. "We are concerned about your INR level."

Eric had his INR level, which indicates how thin the blood is, monitored by Medication Management for some time now. They sometimes made Warfarin dosage changes based on Eric's INR level.

"We believe your INR level needs to be lower for the surgery so that your blood will clot normally after the procedure," the nurse told him. "We are recommending that you take a 'bridge drug' which will allow the INR level to drop enough for the surgery, but not too much."

Eric agreed to take the bridge medication, but that turned out to be a mistake. The bridge medication backfired rather spectacularly. The day after the port was placed in him, Eric woke up to extreme pain in his back. Lorina took him to the emergency room, and after tests and X-rays, the doctors determined that Eric was experiencing a back bleed. The thinned-out blood was hemorrhaging into his back and causing immense pain. Eric was immediately admitted to the hospital and given very strong painkillers to address the back pain. He slept a lot, and remembered waking up from time to time, but Lorina saw it differently.

"It seemed as if you were in a coma for five days," she said. "I was so scared I would lose you. In fact, I'm surprised the doctors managed to bring you back."

Spending so much time lying in bed in one position led to another complication, a major bed sore in the area of Eric's tailbone.

After being released from the hospital, he spent several months going to the hospital wound care center to treat the bed sore. He couldn't sit in one position for any length of time, and while other patients in the infusion center would receive their treatments laying back in a recliner chair, Eric spent his infusion sessions sitting on the edge of his recliner. His mental outlook for the fall was bleak, He wasn't teaching, He wasn't making music, and he was in too much pain to do so.

Chapter 13
A way forward

Eric did a lot of thinking while he was in the hospital. The idea of not teaching was so very hard to accept. At the root of his feelings was the fundamental notion that when he was in front of his classroom, teaching students and rehearsing with them, he was making a difference. He was, in his own way, providing a positive experience in their lives. An experience that they would not only remember well into their adult lives, but one that would shape their development as adults. For many of them, it very well might play a part in fostering success in whatever endeavor they may decide to undertake. Eric would often say, "But now, who am I making a difference with? Nobody!" It was maddening.

Eric kept following the state web site for teacher vacancies, knowing that applying for any of them would not only be impractical, but downright foolish. Then one day his eye caught a posting that drew his attention. A school district, about 45 minutes from his house.

"They're seeking an elementary school band instructor," he told Lorina. "The position is for two mornings a week, and for two hours each morning. Hell, I can do that."

Now, back in the day, when applying for a teaching position, one needed to mail several documents to a prospective employer, a letter of application, a resume, college transcripts, a copy of one's state certification, etc. These days, one does basically the same thing, but the documents need to be submitted online. Not being skilled enough in technology to know how to accomplish these tasks, Eric relied on his son, who was now a music teacher himself, to help him make the initial online application.

As many people who have experienced cancer may know, sometimes one has good days and other times bad days. The morning after Eric applied for the teaching position, he woke up to a bad day, and he realized that he really shouldn't be taking on a job like this after all. It wouldn't be fair to the students, and it wouldn't be fair to the school. So, he decided to take himself out of the running for the position.

However, this episode sparked an idea. When Eric received his new laptop, one of the first things he did was to purchase a Sibelius program. Sibelius is a music writing program. When using it, one could write simple melodies or full-blown orchestrations. When the music was printed, it would produce professional looking notation, as if it were done by a commercial printer. Eric had used Sibelius for many years when he was teaching. There were several years when he directed a small size band, and over the years, developed an ability to orchestrate music for his small groups, making them sound like a bigger ensemble than they actually were. It is difficult to program performance music for a small band. Using commercial band music with them can be very problematic. The reason is that commercial band arrangements are written for bands numbering anywhere from 40 to 80 players. When a small band of, say, 20 players attempts to perform a commercial band selection, it is likely to sound like a musical jigsaw puzzle with many pieces missing. Eric now had the ability to customize arrangements for small groups, giving them a more solid sound.

"If I could use my ability to help directors in a similar situation and give their bands the same advantage that I was able to give mine, I would, in my own little way, be making a difference again," he told Lorina.

He decided to give this idea a try, and called a friend of his, Jonathan, who taught in a small junior-senior high school in a small rural town. It had been a few years since Eric had talked to Jonathan, and they spent the first few minutes of the call catching up. Eric then proposed his idea to him. Jonathan's reaction was immediate.

"That would be great!" Joanathan exclaimed. "I started this position in Deerfield three years ago with a band of just four students. I used small ensemble music with them, and it worked out pretty well. Now, the band has eleven players, but programming for them has become difficult. The ensemble music doesn't work quite as well anymore. Commercial arrangements are a waste of time. The group is just too small. What you're proposing sounds exactly like what I need!"

"Where would you like me to start?" Eric asked.

Jonathan thought for a moment, then said, "How about the 'Tenth Regiment March' by R.B. Hall?"

"Yeah, I can do that," said Eric. "Give me your instrumentation and I'll start work on it tomorrow."

Eric was very familiar with the "Tenth Regiment March," and in fact, had performed it with his own band a couple of times. Although R. B. Hall was considered a Maine composer, and spent most of his time directing Maine bands, he also spent about a year directing the 10th Regiment Military Band of Albany, New York. The group was originally made up of civil war veterans and had fallen on hard times, but with Hall's leadership, the band started to flourish. Hall composed the march just before he left the group. In an interesting twist, when R. B. Hall submitted the march to British publishers, they balked at it. It wasn't that they didn't like the march, but in true British fashion, they considered it unacceptable to publish a march named after an American military unit. They eventually published the march, but under the title "Death and Glory." To erase all doubt, the publishers actually started rumors that R.B. Hall was a British composer.

A week later, Eric sent the completed arrangement to Jonathan. Jonathan loved it and requested additional arrangements. Eric then called another old friend, Jim, who he went to college with. Jim taught in a catholic school, and had a small, but really good band. Jim's request was that Eric update an arrangement that he had written for Jim's band many years ago. Back then, personal computers were not that common, and Eric had hand-written the arrangement. Jim mailed him old copies of the music, and Eric re-did the arrangement on Sibelius. Not only did it come out great, but Eric found a couple of errors that he had made in the original orchestration. Eric was now keeping himself busy for a portion of each day writing music for these bands.

When each of them asked how much they should pay him, Eric told them, "Nothing."

He was starting to feel useful again, and he certainly wasn't going to charge for that.

Chapter 14
More problems

It was late January, and Eric just had the feeling that something wasn't right. It wasn't a problem with the cancer. Having ruled out surgery, when the oncologist put him on his cancer treatment regimen, he told Eric the best they could hope for was to prevent the tumor from growing. The latest CT scan showed that the chemo medications were doing quite well in that regard, and the tumor showed hardly any growth at all. But when Eric checked his weight, he realized that he had lost over a hundred pounds over the last year. Eric had always been overweight as an adult, and 18 months ago, he weighed over 300 pounds. Eric mused that he now had the solution for losing weight.

He could picture a TV commercial with a handsome spokesman smiling into the camera and saying: HI FOLKS, HAVE YOU SPENT YOUR ENTIRE ADULT LIFE OVERWEIGHT? HAVE YOU TRIED DIET AFTER DIET, ONLY TO FIND THAT WHATEVER WEIGHT YOU MIGHT HAVE LOST CAME RIGHT BACK? HAVE YOU TAKEN ON EXERCISE PROGRAMS ONLY TO FIND THAT THEY DIDN'T HELP AT ALL? HAVE I GOT THE SOLUTION FOR YOU! CANCER, THAT'S RIGHT, IF YOU CAN COME DOWN WITH CANCER, YOU'LL SHED THOSE UNWANTED POUNDS IN NO TIME! MILLIONS OF PEOPLE HAVE LOST WEIGHT BY COMING DOWN WITH CANCER AND NOW, YOU CAN BE ONE OF THEM! NO QUESTION! THIS WORKS! JUST CALL THE NUMBER BELOW TO SCHEDULE AN INJECTION OF CANCER CELLS. ALL IT WILL COST YOU IS YOUR LIFE! CALL NOW!

It seemed amusing to Eric anyway. When he spoke to his doctor about how he was feeling, she sent him to the lab for extensive bloodwork. A few days later, he received a call from his kidney doctor. Apparently, all of Eric's doctors had spent the last few days emailing each other, and it seems that the kidney doctor was charged with giving him the bad news.

"The lab results show that your kidneys are going into shutdown," he said.

Eric wasn't surprised. He knew that inevitably this day would come.

Eric had been under a nephrologist's care for 17 years. It started when he went into acute kidney failure. He remembered the day quite clearly. He was with his family in the music building at the University of Maine. His daughter, a high school senior, was auditioning to become a music major. Eric was so proud. Her audition took place in the recital hall, and when she went in for her audition, Eric and his son headed for the stairwell. Eric knew the building well enough to know that there was a back entrance to the recital hall, so they went down the stairs to the back entrance door so they could hear her audition. Sure enough, the sound of her saxophone could be heard clearly through the door as she played her audition piece. She did marvelously, and when she finished, they could hear talking between her and the professor, although Eric couldn't make out what they were saying. Having heard enough, Eric and his son headed back up the stairs to the lobby, where Lorina waited.

As he neared the top of the stairs, Eric's vision started blurring. It felt as if he was going into a major dizzy spell. Eric felt his way along the wall as he walked through the doorway into the lobby. The lobby was crowded with people, but Eric couldn't even see Lorina, or anyone else for that matter. Everything was a blur. He quietly leaned against the nearest wall, and waited, hoping that his vision would clear up. Lorina, sensing something was wrong, came over to him. As they talked, Eric's vision started to clear up. As the family walked back to the car, Eric's son and daughter flanked him, just in case his vision started playing tricks again. Lorina took the wheel, and Eric got into the passenger seat. They drove home, and then right to the hospital emergency room. The doctors there were quick to diagnose the acute kidney failure, and Eric was admitted immediately. The following morning, Eric woke up to find a woman standing at the foot of his hospital bed.

"Good morning," she said to him, "I'm Doctor O'Donnell, your new kidney doctor."

She had a wonderful demeanor, and Eric took an instant liking to her. Dr. O'Donnell told him that he had been diagnosed with kidney disease stage 3, border-line stage 4.

"It's a progressive disease," she explained, "and eventually you will progress to stage 5, at which point you will require kidney dialysis."

Eric was horrified.

"I can't do dialysis," Evan told the doctor, "I'm heavily invested in my job. I'm President of the state music teachers association, and active in the music activities that take place in my district of the state. Music teachers throughout the state are depending on me, and I don't have time to be hooked up to a dialysis machine three times a week. It would be a career ender."

Eric vowed that he would do whatever it would take to avoid that from happening. He saw Dr. O'Donnell regularly for the first few years, but then she retired. He then had Dr. Howe as his nephrologist, but after seven years, she left the practice. He now had Doctor Carpenter as his kidney doctor. Over the 17 years, all three of them knew that Eric vehemently despised the idea of undergoing dialysis. However, now the dreaded moment had arrived.

"You have two choices," the doctor said. "One, you can do nothing, and in a couple of months, you will quietly pass away, or two, you can undertake dialysis treatments, which can extend your life, perhaps significantly."

Eric thought about it for a few seconds. The reason he resisted dialysis for so many years was that he felt it would end his teaching career, but now that his career was over, it didn't really matter. There no longer was any point in resisting it, and how much more harm could it cause? As it was, Eric felt like he had one foot in the grave, and the other on a banana peel. He admitted to Dr. Carpenter that it was time to undergo dialysis, and once again, Eric was admitted to the hospital.

Chapter 15
Dialysis

Even though the pandemic was showing signs of receding, the hospital was still in full blown COVID mode. Lorina was unable to see him as the hospital did not allow any visitors, and although Eric didn't need to wear a mask when he was alone in his room, he needed to keep it by his bedside, and put it on when someone entered. The first thing that had to happen in the hospital was bring Eric's INR level down in order to have the surgical procedure he needed. This took a few days. After all, Eric had learned his lesson from the last time and refused the bridge medication to lower the INR. During this time, he was experiencing kidney shutdown with a vengeance. It was as if his kidneys were saying to him, "You bastard, you made us wait for 17 years, and now we're gonna stick it to you!"

It is normal, in kidney shutdown, to have no appetite, and this was the case with Eric.

"It seems so ironic," Eric said to his nurse, "that I, who always loved food, who always had such a hard time staying on a diet, who couldn't get through the day without the three food groups, peanut butter, chocolate, and pizza, didn't want to eat anything."

When he talked to Lorina on the phone, she said, "Do you realize the hospital has classified you as anorexic?"

"No. I wasn't aware," Eric replied, although he was aware his weight started dropping quickly again.

Finally, they brought Eric in for surgery. It was unclear if his INR had dropped naturally, or if the surgeon decided that since he was in the hospital anyway that treatment options would be readily available should there be blood clotting difficulties. The only thing Eric could remember about the procedure was that the operating room was frigid, a COVID protocol. When he asked about it, he was told that this was done to minimize the chance of infection.

Afterward, Eric was returned to his room, and he decided to wash up in the bathroom. When he saw what he looked like in the mirror when he was shirtless, he was in shock. On one side of his chest was the port for cancer treatment infusions. On the other side was the dialysis catheter, recently installed, two clear plastic lines, one with a red cap, the other with a blue cap.

"Oh Lord," Eric thought. "I look like a Borg drone from 'Star Trek.' This is going to take some getting used to."

The following morning, he was taken to the hospital dialysis clinic for his first dialysis treatment. Eric was aware that dialysis treatments generally last four hours, but the dialysis clinic doctor said to him, "Today's treatment is only going to last two hours, is that OK with you?"

"It certainly is!" replied Eric.

For the first hour, there were no problems. Then, Eric started getting antsy. He started moving his legs, trying not to move the rest of his body. The bedsore that he was still nursing from his last time in the hospital was starting to bother him. By the time they disconnected him at the end of the second hour, Eric was ready to scream.

"Oh lord," he said to his nurse. "Apparently, it takes self-discipline to sit for a four-hour dialysis session, and clearly this is not something I possess, at least not now."

The second session was no better. Again, it was only two hours, but Eric was still having a hard time with it. The third session, Eric just about went crazy. It was in a different room in the clinic, and at least he had a TV to watch, which helped pass the time, but after the second hour, they still had not disconnected him. When Eric asked the nurse, who he had not seen in the other two sessions, she told him that he was scheduled for a four-hour session. The last two hours were way more difficult than the first two, and when the doctor entered the room, Eric called him over to his bed.

"Doctor," he said, "I did not realize that this was supposed to be a four-hour session today and I'm having a real hard time with it. I'm having minor chest pain, and I'm having a really hard time staying still."

"Hmmm," the doctor replied and pressed his palm over Eric's heart. "Is the pain subsiding?" he asked Eric,

"Why, yes, it is," Eric replied. "Thank you doctor."

The doctor stood in thought for a moment, then said, "It looks like you'll be here two more days. I'll make sure those sessions will be two-hour sessions. After that, you'll be released from the hospital, and continue your treatments at the local dialysis clinic."

"Thank you again doctor," said Eric,

"No problem," the doctor replied as he turned to leave.

A few days later, Eric spoke to the head nurse at the local dialysis clinic. As a means of easing him into treatments, Eric would not start out with three four-hour sessions a week. Instead, he would come in for four three-hour sessions a week for the first month. To Eric, that sounded reasonable. The downside- The sessions would start at 6:30 am. Getting up that early four days a week was a challenge, but Lorina was very understanding, and would drive him to each session. They were usually on time. Eric still found the recliner chairs uncomfortable. He had been recently released from the hospital's wound care department, which had been treating the bedsore on his tailbone, but the bedsore still had not completely healed. When it would become too difficult to lay back in the recliner, Eric would sit up on the edge of the chair, which would help although it would set off concern among the clinic staff. Although the sessions were still difficult, Eric noticed that he was tolerating them better.

"Perhaps with time," he thought to himself, "things will get better."

Chapter 16
Time To Be Positive

It was just the local pizza restaurant, but to Eric, it might as well have been a banquet hall. It was time to celebrate. Nothing fancy, just dinner with Lorina, and a few of his former students that were now in college. Jonathan had stopped by also, and so did Paul, taking time from his busy end-of-the-year schedule. After everyone arrived, and orders had been placed, Eric asked for everyone's attention.

"Thank you everyone for coming," he began. "When I was first diagnosed with cancer, I was given a prognosis of less than a year. Today marks the two year anniversary since that awful day, and although I'm still contending with major health issues, I'm doing ok."

Everyone smiled, and Eric continued, "Most of the credit goes to my wife, Lorina, who has acted as my major caregiver through this whole time."

Now it was Lorina's turn to smile.

"For the time being," Eric explained, "the cancer medication my doctor has me on seems very effective. It's showing success, with my latest CT scan showing little or no tumor growth. Not that there haven't been a few setbacks, but either through a medication change, or some other strategy, I have been able to cope. That's also not to say that I'm feeling great. I still have good days and bad days, and I'm still physically limited. It's doubtful that I will ever reach the stage where I can be pronounced 'cured,' and a fully active life is still out of the question. But I'm still holding my own. And I wouldn't be fully honest with you if I didn't admit that dialysis also played a part in this success. You know, I basically was dragged into dialysis kicking and screaming, but now, some bright spots are starting to appear. For one, my appetite has increased so that sometimes, at the end of my sessions, I'm very hungry. I was expecting to see big weight gains. After all, I've lost 140 pounds over the last year and a half, and my wife is starting to complain that I look too thin."

"You better believe it," commented Lorina and Eric laughed.

"In all my adult life, no one ever accused me of being too thin," he responded. "I noticed in my dialysis sessions that my weight was fairly consistent each time I went. I soon learned that as well as cleansing the blood, the dialysis machine also works to eliminate excess fluid in the body. In effect, the dialysis machine was stabilizing my weight. Also, at the end of some of my sessions, I was feeling energized. My wife, who spent decades as a geriatric nurse, can't get over this when she sees it. She says, 'My patients would always crash for the rest of the day when they would do dialysis, what's wrong with you?' I don't have an answer for that, but I have a saying that I have used throughout the years that I've always adhered to: 'Never argue with success!' In addition, my heart function has increased by fifteen points. One of the dialysis nurses told me that when you have a dialysis session, the effect on your heart is as if you were walking for four hours."

Eric paused for a moment, looking at his former students. "And as long as I'm being honest, I also have to admit I miss teaching terribly. I miss conducting the rehearsals, I miss the performances, I miss planning the spring trips, but most of all," he paused as he started to choke up, "I miss Bay Shore High School."

"And we miss you!" Paul added.

Eric had to pause again, but he continued on, "Well, I can't walk into a classroom and teach. I don't know if I'll ever be able to, but I like to think that the music I write for various school groups has had a positive effect on those students. When I started writing for Jonathan's band, the group consisted of 11 students. It now has grown to 25, and I like to think I played a role in that."

"You most certainly did!" responded Jonathan.

"I'm glad," said Eric. "You know, I never imagined that I would have such an active schedule when I retired. My days are filled with dialysis treatments, cancer treatments, doctors' visits, blood tests and scans of all kinds. It's very rare that I have a day with nothing scheduled, but that doesn't mean that I can't enjoy things as they come. I'm still involved in music, a little orchestrating and a little performing. In the summertime, I perform with a couple of community bands. I have a new toy for this. I picked it up on eBay, a 1911 Carl Fischer Mellophonium."

Eric responded to the many quizzical looks, "It's kind of like a french horn, but with trumpet valves."

Everyone seemed satisfied with his explanation.

After a pause, Eric said, "Well, I think I've talked enough. Everyone, enjoy your meal, and I hope I get a chance to talk with each of you."

As the meal progressed, Eric was able to speak with just about everyone. But his most memorable conversation was with one of his former students who said to him, "Mr. Matthews, you seem to have gone through a lot over the last few years. How did you manage it without going crazy?"

Eric sat back and thought about it for a moment.

"Well," he said, "I think it probably has a lot to do with what I used to tell you guys in marching band. It's all about how you manage the transitions."

-End